My Brother's Keeper 2

Love, Lies & Betrayal

Tina J

Copyright 2018

More Books by Tina J

A Thin Line Between Me & My Thug 1-2
I Got Luv for My Shawty 1-2
Kharis and Caleb: A Different kind of Love 1-2
Loving You is a Battle 1-3
Violet and the Connect 1-3
You Complete Me
Love Will Lead You Back
This Thing Called Love
Are We in This Together 1-3
Shawty Down to Ride For a Boss 1-3
When a Boss Falls in Love 1-3
Let Me Be The One 1-2
We Got That Forever Love
Ain't No Savage Like The One I got 1-2
A Queen & Hustla 1-3 (collab)
Thirsty for a Bad Boy 1-2
Hasaan and Serena: An Unforgettable Love 1-2
We Both End Up With Scars
Caught up Luvin a beast 1-3
A Street King & his Shawty 1-2
I Fell for the Wrong Bad Boy 1-2 (collab)
Addicted to Loving a Boss 1-3
All Eyes on the Crown 1-3
I Need that Gangsta Love 1-2 (collab)
Still Luvin' a Beast 1-2
Creepin' With The Plug 1-2
I Wanna Love You 1-2
Her Man, His Savage 1-2
When She's Bad, I'm Badder 1-3
Marco & Rakia 1-3
Feenin' for a Real One 1-3
A Kingpin's Dynasty 1-3
What Kind Of Love Is This?
Frankie & Lexi 1-3
A Dope Boy's Seduction 1-3
My Brother's Keeper 1-3

Previously…

Rakim

"What's up with your pussy?" I asked Jocelyn after we finished having sex. I'm telling you that ever since the day we slept together a few weeks ago, I been seeing her a lot more.

After she beat Talia up for telling Ranisha about us, I felt relieved because it meant she wouldn't tell my business to Jocelyn. Talia had a lotta growing up to do and if she ever planned on getting a man, she better keep her legs closed and stop tryna mess with other people's men.

Hell, to this day, friends or not, I could probably still fuck her. I'm not saying my dick is all that, I'm lying; yes, I am. She's most likely heard the stories and wanna taste but I'm good. She's the type to get strung and become a stalker.

"Ain't shit wrong with my pussy." She got offended and rose to her feet and began getting dressed.

We were at my spot because she resided with her brother. I don't have a problem showing my face there but she wants to wait. It's crazy because she's the only woman who has ever been in this house and we aren't even a couple. The reason why is because I'm still fucking Ranisha and if she found out, what could she say?

I told Ranisha on the phone a few times not to hit me up anymore and for the first few days she listened. However, I stopped by because she was crying about taking her life and BAM! I fucked her and haven't stopped. I told her Jocelyn is my main and if she ever said a word to her or Talia, I would never fuck with her again. Since she's a money hungry chick, she agreed.

Before anyone talks shit, I am not in a relationship and free to do me. And HELL NO! Jocelyn can't sleep with anyone else. Call it unfair all you want, it's what the fuck I say.

"Don't be offended ma." I put my boxers on and stood

behind her.

"I'm asking because it feels different and…" She

covered her mouth and her eyes grew big.

"What?"

"No, I can't be." She started pacing back and forth,

panicking. Her phone started to ring on the nightstand.

"Hold on. This is the GYN office." I shrugged my

shoulders because I knew she went to get put on birth control.

We were fucking like rabbits on a regular and sometimes I

pulled out and other times, I didn't. Neither of us were ready

for kids and decided we had to be more careful, which is why I

pulled out today.

"Hello." She said, the lady asked if Jocelyn wanted her

results over the phone. I didn't know they did that but after hearing her relay her personal information, I guess they can. She spoke to the woman for a few minutes.

"Are you sure?" She gave me an evil look.

"I'm positive, it's only been one sex partner. The test results are 100% correct, right?" She asked again.

"Oh my God. Can you repeat that for me please? I wanna make sure I heard you correctly." She put the phone on speaker.

"Ms. Alvarado, you are pregnant." Damn, she got pregnant fast as hell. No wonder it felt different. I've never felt a woman's pussy pregnant but I can say its feels even more amazing.

"You have contracted a disease known as Trichomoniasis. We've contacted your local pharmacy to fill the prescription for you." *What the fuck did the bitch just say?*

"Thank you. I'll go pick it up."

"Also, please contact your sexual partner and inform him too." Each time the woman spoke, Jocelyn was getting angrier and I don't blame her. I know she wasn't fucking anyone else, so if she did have something, it came from me.

"How is this disease transmitted?"

"The internet will tell you it comes from many things but the truth is, it comes from having unprotected sex with someone who has it."

"Thank you."

"Ms. Alvarado, we would like you to come in to get bloodwork and test you for the more serious diseases such as HIV, Chlamydia, Hepatitis and Herpes." I could see Jocelyn breaking down.

To hear, I gave her something and now she had to be tested for other diseases, is fucked up. Shit, I had to get my ass tested now too. I really messed up. When she gets off this phone, I bet she's gonna curse me the fuck out.

"I'll be there tomorrow." She ended the call with the woman and gave me a hateful stare.

"*I'm not sleeping with anyone but you Jocelyn. No one can fuck me like you Jocelyn. You better not fuck no one else Jocelyn.*" She recited all the things I said to her as she began crying harder.

"You know Rakim, I beat Talia's ass because she told me you had a girlfriend and I defended you. There's no way you could when we spent so much time together but I was wrong." She put her sneakers on.

"I refuse to ask, how could you because you're the exact type of nigga I thought you were, which is why I stayed away from you." I couldn't say a damn thing because she was right about everything. We may not have been a couple but I damn sure told her not to mess with anyone else.

"Jocelyn, we weren't a couple and…"

BAM! She threw the lamp at me off the nightstand and it broke in pieces. I tried to get over to her but she held her hand out for me to stay away.

"Don't you fucking dare patronize me with your bullshit." I felt like shit seeing her cry harder.

"You fucked some bitch or bitches raw dog and have the nerve to tell me, we weren't a couple." I knew exactly when it happened too.

Like I said, Ranisha called me over and we ended up fucking without a condom. I never came in her and pulled out before my precum leaked out. If the bitch gave me something, it means she raw dogging everyone. Not that I care because it's my fuck up but damn. How could I give her a disease? I ain't never had anything in my life, so hell yea, I'm pissed.

"We may not have been a couple as you say, but I was still faithful to your dog ass. What was I thinking tryna be with a hood nigga? I should've stayed alone, had I known this would happen. She started putting the rest of her clothes on.

"Say, I wanted to keep this baby Rakim. Do you have any idea what type of damage it could've done to the child?"

"What you mean if?" She stormed past me and down the steps. I didn't want a kid but she's not getting rid of it either. We knew the precautions.

"I'm not ready for a kid."

"But you were with the other nigga?" I rushed down the steps and caught her at the door.

"Benji and I had years in Rakim. We got weeks and in this short amount of time, I caught something from you.

12

Whether Benji was faithful or not, he never, ever brought me back anything; not even a fucking cold." She snatched her keys and phone off the bed.

"Look, we were just fucking right, so there's no need to keep a child when the parents aren't even gonna be together."

"Tha fuck you mean we aren't gonna be together?"

"Please tell me you're not one of those niggas who thinks he can do what he wants and the chick can't."

"Jocelyn, don't play with me." She opened the door and scoffed up a laugh.

"I don't have to play with you anymore because the person who probably gave you the disease is here." She went to walk out and I followed. Ranisha was getting out her car and headed in my direction.

"What the fuck you doing here and how you find out where I lived?"

"While your ass is over here playing house with this bitch, I need money to pay some bills. And why haven't you ever invited me here?" I don't think she expected Jocelyn to punch her in the face because I damn sure didn't. Ranisha tried to run after Jocelyn who smirked and stopped to see what she'd do.

"Have a nice life Rakim and make sure you handle that because I'm setting my appointment up ASAP."

"You better stop playing with me Jocelyn."

"FUCK YOU! DIRTY DICK ASS NIGGA!" She hopped in her car fast as hell and peeled out.

I ran in the house to get dressed, forgetting Ranisha was even here. I threw my clothes on put my phone in my pocket and ran down the steps. This bitch had the nerve to come out my kitchen eating a banana.

"Bitch, you gave me something." I barked walking in her direction.

"I didn't give you shit."

"My girl just got off the phone with her doctor. She has Trich or some shit." I had to think about what I said. Did I just call Jocelyn my girl?

"Oh, that's nothing. I had it a few times. The doctor will give you medicine and…" I didn't even let the bitch finish and punched her in the face. Her body slid down the wall.

I don't care what any readers say about beating up a chick. My momma raised me better than to put my hands on a woman, but Ranisha deserved it. She knew she had the shit and whether I was wrong or not for fucking her, she had no business not telling me or even letting me fuck her raw.

I grabbed her hair and drug her out the front door. Imagine my surprise when I opened it and this bitch was

15

standing there grinning. How in the hell is everyone finding out where I live? I've never let a woman come here unless it was family and now Jocelyn, but today everyone stopping through.

"How the fuck are you here?" I asked Nika and saw Dash speeding in my driveway. Did he know she was out and had her meet over here?

"Somehow Darrell, took all the weight and said he forced me into robbing banks." She stepped over Ranisha and in my house.

"The judge had pity on me, you know especially; after hearing my son was gonna be snatched away from my cousin."

"Get the fuck out Nika."

"What the hell is going on and how the hell did you know where my brother lived?" Dash and I both stood there as she plopped on the couch. Ranisha was on the porch moaning about her face hurting. I slammed the door and waited for Nika

to speak.

"I'm only here to see where my son will live."

"Why the hell would your son live here?" I asked and

she stood smirking.

"Rakim, Rakim, Rakim." She waved her ugly ass index

finger and came closer. This bitch better not say, what I think

she's gonna say.

"Dash, I see your brother didn't tell you, so let me be

the first."

"BITCH, GET OUT!" I went to force her and my

brother stopped me.

"Tell me what?" My phone started ringing as she spoke

and it was my mother. I let it go to voicemail.

"The little boy you think is yours, is really Rakim's."

The phone fell out my hand and chaos took over.

Jose

I walked in the house, tossed my keys on the table and ran upstairs to shower. Ever since I found out someone's been watching Mari, I've wrecked my brain daily tryna figure out who. Her brother Levi, tapped into the security camera and found the person who sent the message. Unfortunately, he told Dash, who is supposed to drop by later and tell me.

"What you doing here?" I asked Talia who had the nerve to be lying in my bed, naked and watching television.

"Your sister let me in."

"Bullshit!" Jocelyn and Mari were cool as hell and regardless; of our situation right now, my sister wouldn't dare let Talia in.

"I'm serious. Go ask." She offered and I did just that.

I knocked on Jocelyn's door and there was no answer. I cracked it and she too laid on the bed; only difference is tears were coming down her face. I ran over to check and see if everything is ok.

I didn't expect her to hand me a damn positive pregnancy test. Well she gave me the paper with the results on it. I don't believe she's ready for a kid with Benji but fuck it. I'm about to be an uncle and a nigga excited as hell.

"I'm not keeping it." There goes my excitement.

"Why not?"

"He gave me a disease." I hopped out off the bed.

"A disease?"

"It wasn't AIDS or anything like that and it's been treated but still. He told me I couldn't be with anyone and he went out and slept around."

"Sis, you knew Benji was with the stripper chick."

"Benji? This isn't Benji's baby."

"Huh? I'm confused."

19

She started telling me about this guy she kept dodging because he was into the streets. Even with avoiding him, he found her at school, they hooked up and been together ever since. It's crazy because I knew she had someone occupying her time, I just assumed it was Benji tryna make up. Who knew there was another man?

"Who is the guy? Wait! Did you tell him about the baby and I hope you at least told him to get checked out?" Whether he cheated and gave her something or not, it's her responsibility to fill him in on both things.

The crazy thing is, I've heard women discuss how they wouldn't tell the guy if he gave her something because he knew he slept with a chick unprotected. I understood but men don't always get symptoms like women.

"How long you gonna be Jose, I'm horny?" I heard and turned around to see this trick in my damn robe.

"You back to messing with her?" The second my sister asked, I knew Talia crept in somehow.

"HELL NO! You know who my girl is. She said, you let her in." Jocelyn sat up.

"I had no idea she was here. You know I wouldn't do Mari like that." I should've know better.

"How the fuck you get in?"

"The back door was unlocked." She had a huge grin on her face.

"That means you jumped the fence." Jocelyn said.

"You desperate as fuck yo!" I was mad as hell and so was my sister.

"Bitch, you gotta go." I grabbed her arm and pushed her out the room. I had her pick her things up and if my luck couldn't get worse, the doorbell rang. I stared at the monitor that shows outside and it was Mari. Talia ran down the steps

21

naked before I could catch her. Mad isn't the word for the way I'm feeling.

"Well looky here." Talia opened the door and the look on Mari's face was disgusted and disappointing.

"Mari this is not what it looks like."

"It's ok Jose. You told me we weren't together so I expected it but did it have to be her?" I know they saw one another at the diner that one time but were they affiliated with one another before?

"That's right bitch. Another one bites the dust."

"What is she talking about and put your fucking clothes on? Tryna make her think we fucked." I pushed her out the way.

"Jose don't pretend you weren't just making me scream your name. I mean, my pussy juices are still dripping down.

See." This bitch really opened her legs. She must've been playing with herself before I got here.

"Yuk." I heard my sister from upstairs.

"Jocelyn you knew about her being here? Damn, I thought we were cool." Mari turned to leave and Talia kept taunting her.

"I know you love the way his dick curves and he can make you cum multiple times. I know damn well I do. Shit, why you think I won't leave him alone?"

"Shut the fuck up yo."

"Nah. Let her go home crying like the spoiled brat she is. Ho, thinks because her brothers got this town on lock no one can say shit to her." I mushed the hell outta her.

"You say that and here you are sack chasing a nigga who won't claim you." That must've pissed Talia off because she hock spit on Mari and she lost it. It took me a few times to get Mari off her. She was fucking her up and it's exactly what she gets. Mari pushed me off her and damn near ran to her car.

"Mari, I swear she and I didn't fuck. I wouldn't do that to you." She swung her body around.

"I stopped by because I missed you Jose."

"I miss you too Mari and I wanna be with you but it's some things going on that..." I stopped in the middle of my sentence when a black SUV with tinted windows pulled up.

"Didn't I tell you to stay away from him?" The door opened.

"Is this motherfucker serious?" Mari appeared to be shocked and she should be.

"YO! WHY THE FUCK ARE YOU HERE?" I shouted, pissed more than anything.

"She didn't take heed to my warning so we about to set

it off out this bitch." I heard a few guns cock and grabbed Mari.

What type of shit is this?

Efrain

"Where's the product Efrain?" Gavin asked when I was leaving the store. There were a few people in the parking lot but at this time of night, no one really paid attention. I guess when it's a twenty-four-hour spot, people wanna be in and out.

"My brother has it." His two goons slammed me against the wall. I didn't even know his punk ass had anyone who liked him. He was a dick and thought his shit didn't stink. Pretending to be a boss nigga and runs in the face of danger. Let me rewind and go back to how we met.

Gavin and I went to school together and he was the most popular guy. He had that mixed breed complexion. You know the light skinned, good hair, pretty eyes, all that. He never played sports because he claimed to be too cool for them.

26

However; he always threw the best damn parties. There would be ho's for days, alcohol, drugs, and whatever else you can think of that kids have there.

Anyway, we were introduced by this chick I called my girlfriend. She was pretty and big boned. I loved women with meat on their bones. It usually meant she can cook her ass off and had some banging ass pussy.

Nevertheless, we were together for a year before she asked to start attending Gavin's events. If you went to our school, anybody who is somebody is always there and my girl wanted to go. Me, I didn't give a fuck because my whole family was popular and once we got together so was she.

Mari and Rakim hated her because they said she was only using me. If anyone knew Rakim, they knew he didn't like anyone so his thoughts got nowhere in my head. Being a dumb teenager in love, I paid their opinions no mind.

Long story short, I regret not listening because tryna

support my girl, I ended up getting caught up drinking,

smoking weed and dabbling in other shit, here and there.

My graduation was fucked up and so was the party my

parents threw afterwards. I never planned on getting that

fucked up. The party was cleared out by my brother Dash and

everyone left; including my girl. She never even said goodbye

but at the time, nothing mattered to me anyway.

My father had, had enough and sat me down sober the

next day with my mother and asked what the fuck I had going

on. Once I told them, my mom was devastated and my father

was angrier with me for not telling, that he stopped speaking to

me for a few days.

Unfortunately; two weeks prior, something detrimental

happened to me due to being intoxicated and I couldn't handle

it. The entire situation began taking over my mind and

common sense. I drank more, sniffed a little more, could care

less if I lived or died, and the nightmares are still constant. Had

it not been for my mom checking up on me, every fucking hour

of the day, I probably would've killed myself a long time ago.

My parents want me to attend therapy but talking to

someone doesn't make shit go away. It only reminds you of the

chaos and if I'm tryna block it out, why would I talk about it?

It's the exact reason, I've been MIA recently. I've been on the

hunt to rid myself of the problem. The only reason I even fuck

with Gavin at this point is because he's blackmailing me,

otherwise; I would never do any sort of business with him.

Long story short, he had me selling dope for him in

order to remain quiet about my ordeal. Evidently, it's on video

and he has it. Of course, I didn't believe him until he showed it

to me. I tried to take his life but he had no issue informing me

the video is on his father's computer at his job. Now, ain't no way in hell I'm getting into a Wall Street office, therefore; I'm stuck with this dumb ass.

"Why does your brother have it?" He knew exactly who my family is, so why even ask? This the dumb shit I be talking about.

"When I was outta town, my mom brought me a new place. My brothers came in and removed it."

"Well, my boss beat my ass for giving you a package that you didn't hand deliver to the correct person like you were supposed to."

"Not my problem." I tossed the cigarette at his feet.

"That's where you're wrong." He nodded to one of the dudes who appeared to be skeptical about being here.

"You see, my people's here is gonna bestow the same beatdown on you, that my boss gave me."

"Well, I hope your boss knows he fucking with a coward." I moved closer.

"Someone whose blackmailing another in order to make his own money off the product." Gavin's mouth dropped. What he didn't know was I knew he wasn't this big boss and whoever is in charge, has no idea this nigga making side deals with people. He'd get the product from whoever, sell it to the person for almost triple the price and keep the money.

For those who don't understand; if the product is $500, he'd sell it to those people for $1500 and sometimes even higher. Of course, his boss couldn't be aware because he'd probably make him pay up and all Gavin's doing, is having customers look elsewhere. When a product is high, you can believe the customer will go out and find a better deal. His ass will learn eventually. If I knew who his boss was, I'd rat his ass out.

"You cost me money Efrain because I had to pay the customer his money and repay the boss."

"Why do you keep calling him boss, if you're the boss?" I stood there with my arms folded.

"He's the supplier and I have workers under me." I gave him the side eye.

"Look nigga, I'm not here to answer dumb questions. Get his ass." The dude swung off and knocked me off balance.

"That's all you got?" I caught dude in the face, swept his feet and he was down. The other guy jumped in as I punched and banged his head in the ground. I felt him punch me on the side of my head and this time, it dazed the hell outta me.

My body fell to the side and the kicks and punches were landing all over me. I looked up and saw a bat, out the corner of my eye. Tryna get outta the way, nothing prepared

32

me for the metal bat going across my back. The pain was unbearable and I knew, my ass would be laid up. Still, not letting these niggas get the best of me, I rolled over the best I could and staggered to my feet. I wiped the blood out my eyes and saw someone who I least expected coming in my direction.

"Efrain, is that you?" He yelled coming out the store. I could tell he was on the phone by the way his head tilted to the side.

"GO!!!!" I yelled as loud as I could but he continued walking in my direction. He had no idea the shit he walked into until it was too late.

"Who the fuck are you?" And just like that Gavin hit him over the head with the bat. George went down and his body started shaking. I lifted the other security dude up, slammed him on his neck and kicked him in the ribs, the best I could. My vision was getting worse and I could no longer stand.

33

As my body slid down the car, someone lifted me up from

behind and wrapped a wire around my neck.

Dashier

My phone constantly rang from an unknown number.
Usually, I don't answer them on the weekend because most
likely it's about work anyway. However, this number called at
least six times already, which made me believe the call was
indeed important.

Now I'm aggravated because I was supposed to leave
today and go pick my son and Genesis up. Unfortunately, I
hadn't spoken to Rakim or Efrain all day and both of them
wanted to tag along. Demaris was still struggling with the Jose
being crazy situation and decided to greet us when we returned.

The excitement between myself, Kingston and Genesis
had been built up for over a week. Not saying we weren't
happy prior to, but now that it's closer to the actual day, the
momentum is greater. I think Genesis was more excited for us
to meet than anything. Evidently, she had friends who grew up
without a father and didn't want the same for my son. I
appreciated her taking great care of him and planned on

compensating her. Four years is a long time and from the way I see it, she deserves it.

"HELLO!" I barked in my phone as I continued packing an overnight bag. My intentions were to grab them and return immediately, but my son had other plans. He wanted us to see a few places in the morning before hopping the flight home.

"Why are you shouting?" I looked down at my phone again to make sure I was hearing her right. How the hell did this bitch get my number and why is she even calling?

"What Nika?" I carried on with what I was doing. I didn't wanna miss the flight.

"I thought you'd be happy to hear I'm home and..." I ceased all movement.

"Home? How the fuck are you outta jail?"

"Meet me at your brother Rakim's spot and we can discuss it."

"Why in the hell are you going there and how do you even know where he lives?" Instead of answering, the phone disconnected.

I called Rakim and there was no answer, which made me rush to my car and speed over there. Avoiding all lights and stop signs, I made it at the same time she did. Rakim had Ranisha by the hair and Nika walked in. He appeared to be shocked she's there too.

I hopped out and went in to find her taunting my brother about some shit. However, my mind went into overdrive with her last statement.

"The little boy you think is yours, is really Rakim's." It took me a second to realize Nika had a serious look on her face. Rakim didn't make it better by not responding and his mouth hanging open.

"First of all, you stupid bitch." I had Nika pushed against the wall with my gun to her temple. Hell yea, I brought it. I didn't trust her one bit.

"I took a DNA and the results didn't come back at 80% or even 90%. They were 99.999999 percent which means no one else can possibly be his father. What I wanna know is, how you can suggest Rakim in the first place." I wasn't playing stupid by a long shot.

It don't take a rocket scientist to realize at some point, they slept together. I more or so wanted to hear it. She looked at Rakim and didn't say a word. This bitch had a whole lot to say a minute ago; now she's mute.

"Keep talking bitch. You brought the shit up so speak on it." Tears were streaming down her face.

"You tough. Say it." I cocked the gun back and waited.

"Dash, I don't care if you kill her but let me explain. It wasn't what she's making it seem." I let her go, tossed her to the floor and kicked her hard as hell in the stomach. I kneeled down in front of her.

"That's for keeping my son away all these years." She was crying harder.

"Be happy that's all I'm doing." I stood and turned to my brother.

"Did you fuck her?" Rakim had his hands up as I pointed the gun at him.

"Dash."

"DID YOU FUCK HER?" I shouted again. Complete silence. There's only one thing left to do.

I hit him over the head with the butt of my gun, splitting his eye. My brother is no slouch so when he charged at me, I expected it, which is why I caught him in the ribs. He hunched over and staggered, but hit me with a body shot that had me doing the same thing. At this point, we were going blow for blow.

"STOP THIS SHIT, RIGHT NOW!" I heard my mom yell and we froze. I looked and blood was all over the ground and on both of us.

"You two over here carrying on like some got damn teenagers, when your brother is laid up in the fucking hospital, along with George."

"WHAT?" Both of us shouted out.

"Something happened to Efrain and somehow George was there too." Neither of us said a word.

"Is someone gonna help me up?" Nika asked still lying in a fetal position. I walked over but my mother grabbed my arm.

"Get your trifling ass up and don't let me catch you around my family again." Nika remained quiet and stood on her own. I guess she knew not to fuck with my mom.

"When my son gets here, I will be requesting full custody." This time I had to keep my mom from attacking her. I wasn't even worried because by the time my lawyer is through with her, she'll wanna forget her body even pushed out a child. I went to the door, looked at Rakim and shook my head.

It's not even like I give two shits about Nika now but it's the principle. It's not as if she were a jump off or something. She was the woman I planned on marrying and have all my kids with. It may have turned out different but still.

"I'm out."

"Dash." He said my name and I continued walking. He and I had no words for one another, so I'm not gonna pretend as if I wanna converse about the situation. I headed to my car, sat down and pulled off. I don't care what the reason, he had no business fucking her.

****

I arrived in Alabama on schedule because regardless of the shit I had to deal with at home, I had to get him before Nika did some off the wall shit. I can't and won't take the chance of her fleeing with my son and I really never see him again.

For someone who just got released from jail, she looked good. If I didn't know, I'd say she never did a day behind bars. I knew her body was still decent when she unzipped her jumpsuit tryna fuck, but the tight clothes revealed her sexy shape. Too bad she's not a woman I'd ever bed again and that's not even after hearing about her and my brother. I still can't get over that shit. It's one thing to try and rob my father's bank but she overstepped sleeping with family.

I know Nika coming to see me after being released had nothing to do with exposing her little secret. She's returned for a reason and I'm sure time will reveal her hidden agenda.

I grabbed my small duffel bag from the conveyor belt and made my way outside to find Genesis. I couldn't wait to hold my son and from his reactions over the phone, he felt the same.

I still can't believe I had a four-year-old. I'm not even gonna say I felt, I had a son or daughter out there because Nika made it clear I had nothing to do with making this child. And with her having an affair it was no reason for me to challenge it.

Yea, even though she refused to see me, I visited the jail tryna get her to tell me but I wasn't pressed. Had I been, I may not have lost as much time. *What am I saying?* This is all her fault and she's the blame. I'm not about to regret my choices because she failed to mention him.

I stepped out the airport expecting to see my son and Genesis but no one was there. I glanced around thinking I went past them but nothing. I called her phone and surprisingly; it went to voicemail.

I sat in one of the chairs waiting and sent a text to Levion checking on George and my brother. I was in such a rush to leave so Nika didn't get here first, I never made the stop over at the hospital.

Me: *I'm sorry, I couldn't be there but I had to get here before that dumb bitch pops up. How's George and Efrain?*

Levion: *He's good so far. We still waiting on Efrain to wake up.*

Me: *Does George know anything?*

Levi: *Just that he came out the store and some guys were beating on Efrain. When he went to ask if Efrain was ok, someone attacked him from behind.*

Me: *I'll be there as soon as I get back.*

Levi: *Dash, I know you'd be here if it weren't for anything else. Get my nephew and bring him home. We missed a lotta time with him.*

Me: *I will. Tell George I'm glad he's up and he WILL NOT BE SPOILING HIM!* I put in all capitals. Ever since we found out, George couldn't wait to meet him too. Talking about him and Mari are going to have him all the time.

Levi: *He's laughing, which is good because this is the first time since he's woke up. Hurry up back bro and be careful. If you need me, I'll hop the next flight.*

Me: *I'm good. See y'all tomorrow and call me the minute Efrain opens his eyes.* I hit send and called Genesis phone again and still no answer. I went over to the rent a car place, waited for them to give me the truck and drove to her house.

I assumed she was running late but imagine my surprise when I pulled up and there were two black SUV's full of niggas. I called Benji's brother Raphael, to see if he still had people out here that get dirty. He told me yes, and to wait because they're coming.

Of course, he did some dirty shit on the side and worked with just as many crooked people in the corporate world.

WHOOP! WHOOP! I turned my head and there were six police cars, two detective trucks and a big bouncer looking dude.

"You Dashier?" One of the guys asked when he came to the side of my truck.

"Yea."

"Raphael sent us. We're here for whatever you need." I had to give it to my boy. I expected to see hood niggas, but cops are even better.

I stepped out the truck and walked to the porch. Some of the dudes rose to their feet as others, ice grilled the fuck outta me and the cops.

"Is Genesis here?" One of them looked me up and down.

"Who the fuck looking for her?" I chuckled at this fake ass wanna be thug in front of me. All I did was ask a question and he already talking shit. Why couldn't he just say something like, *yes who's looking for her?* It always gotta be more to it.

"And you are?" I questioned and retuned the same stare down.

"It doesn't matter who I am. Why you rolling up with pigs is the real question?"

"Like you said, it doesn't matter who you are, just like it doesn't matter who I'm rolling with. Excuse me." I went to move around and he tried to steal me. I dodge and laid him the fuck out on the ground.

"YOOOOOOO!" I heard another guy say and they all attempted to come for me. Once those guns clicked, hands went up and niggas backed up.

"Like I was saying. I'm here for Genesis." I opened the front door and shit going on before my eyes, took me to a place I haven't been in a long time. Shit, my own brother didn't even receive this treatment. This motherfucker better hope I don't kill him.

Genesis

I woke up early this morning to get Kingston ready to meet his father and hopefully leave this life of hell behind me. This Dashier guy, purchased me a condo to stay in for a month to appease the court system. We both knew, he'd have his son the entire time but we did what we had to, in order for Kingston to be with his family. Real quick, let me rewind and explain how I ended up with him.

My father and her mother are siblings and we are their only children. They weren't close and stopped speaking to each other quote often. We didn't have a huge family and basically all we got. After my grandmother passed about ten years ago, my father moved us to Alabama. He tried to his sister to come but she refused.

My cousin Nika, has always be the outgoing and go getter between the two of us. Anyway, she got in a relationship with this Dash character. From what my aunt says, he gave her any and everything she wanted. Worshipped the ground she walked on and asked her if he could marry Nika. He went the old-fashioned route and to me it was romantic. I thought they had the perfect love story.

Nika has always been a big ass liar and it's unfortunate she did so much, for attention. We never got the chance to meet him because after speaking to Dash, I was told, she claimed not to have any family besides her mother. The only way you would catch her telling the truth, is if you were there with her when she said, whatever it was took place

Long story short, her dumb ass cheated, got arrested for robbing banks and sent to jail. For some reason she claimed not to know who the father was and didn't want him going to my parents because of their age. Of course, I had no objection in keeping him. He needed to stay with family and not get lost in the system.

For years, I asked Nika who his father was and told her to get her ex Dash tested just in case. Each time she declined and forbid me to do it. I couldn't, if I wanted because my ass had no idea who he was. I had no last name, previous address or anything, But here we are, four years later, about to unite them together and this stupid nigga doing everything to stop the process.

"Where the fuck you going?" Manny asked as I packed a duffle bag. I had money saved in the bank from working so I'd get more clothes when I arrived. I'm also gonna look for a place to stay.

"I told you, Kingston is meeting his father." He smacked me so got damn hard, my nose bled. Instead of basking in my tears like usual, I got up off the floor, and went in the bathroom to clean up. I was on a schedule and didn't wanna be late.

"That's my fucking son Genesis." I snapped my neck to look at him.

He and I been together for three years and he loved Kingston. He took him for haircuts, parties with his family and everything else.

I understand being separated is gonna be hard on him but the fact remains that he's not the father. We even had this discussion with his family and they too are upset but understand. He's the only one who's taking it hard. It's not like

49

Kingston called him daddy and his mom asked him, if that was his kid wouldn't he want the same. We all know a real man, won't allow another to raise his child. Manny doesn't seem to understand.

"Look, Dash is waiting for us at the airport."

"Dash? Oh, now you want the nigga, I see."

"What does me saying his name have to do with anything?"

"*Dash is waiting at the airport.*" He mocked me in a women's voice.

"Are you jealous?" I stormed past and finished packing. Each item I put in, he took out.

Manny is the poster child for being bi-polar. Like most relationships, we were perfect in the beginning. No fighting, arguing; nothing.

Over the last two years, he's changed a lot. He started cheating and became more violent. He's never hit me until just now but the verbal abuse has been horrible. Unfortunately, he cursed me out so many times in front of Kingston, that he became scared of him too.

"Jealous of what? He can't do shit for you." I smiled on the inside because he had no idea what Dashier could do. I'd never ask for anything but he didn't know that.

"You're right?" I left the bag, went in Kingston's room to grab him and went down the stairs. His temper is rising so the best thing to do is get outta here and fast. I can get clothes from Walmart or a mall out there.

"Oh you think he's gonna fuck you." I stopped in my tracks.

"Kingston sit in the living room." He ran off.

"I don't want a man my cousin has been with. Manny look." I grabbed my purse and phone. There were text messages from Dash asking where we were and he tried calling too.

"I'm taking him to Jersey and returning in a few weeks."

"If you come back pregnant, I'm gonna kill you."

"Pregnant? Where the hell did that come from?" He was really bugging right now and I needed to get away from him before things escalated.

"Oh wait! Your insides are fucked up and won't even let a baby roast in there for longer than two months." I gasped and covered my mouth as the tears cascaded down my face. He hit below the belt and he knew because he stood there smirking.

He and I, were trying to have our own baby for the last two years. Unfortunately; I couldn't carry past two months for some reason. The doctor had no idea why, however; my mom said, it's because God doesn't want me to have a baby with him. The constant cheating took a toll on my body. I never told the doctor about the stress but after looking online for answers, he pretty much is responsible for me losing all three.

"Who the fuck is that?" He asked and I went to the window. I only saw a guy in a truck.

"Who is who and why are all those guys in my yard?" They were standing on the porch and some were drinking by the trucks.

"Because I told them they could come."

"Manny, make them leave."

"Hell no. We about to party in here when you bounce." He grabbed a beer out the fridge and leaned against the wall watching me. I wasn't even about to argue or debate anything with him. I shook my head, called Kingston and was about to open the door when I felt my hair being pulled.

"Let go of her. Let go." I heard Kingston saying. I looked and he was kicking Manny. I cried because this man was attacking me and my little cousin is trying to help. How can a 4-year-old know what to do?

"Move Kingston." Manny barked.

"Go in the other room Kingston." I cried out because I didn't want him to get hurt.

"No. Let Genny go." That's what he called me.

"Move it lil nigga." He gripped my hair tighter and almost snapped my neck to force me to look at him.

"You better be home in 2 weeks." He pushed me against the wall and my face slammed into it. I slid down and my vision started to get blurry.

"Awww shit." He yelled out. I don't know what Kingston did but outta nowhere I saw Kingston's body go in the air from the kick Manny gave him.

Next thing I know, someone came in the door and started beating the crap outta Manny. I struggled to my feet, ran over to Kingston and noticed blood trickling from his nose. The kick was hard but luckily, he ended on the edge of the couch. He did hit his head on the floor and it bounced off like a ball, but we had a rug so it didn't hit as hard. Don't get me wrong the floor is still hard but a rug had a little cushion.

"Please help me." I ran out the house and cops were everywhere. Where the hell did they come from and who called them?

"What happened to him?" One of the officers grabbed Kingston from me and placed him in the car.

"My boyfriend was fighting me and he tried to step in. He kicked him and he hit his head. Drive faster please." I was screaming and kissing all over his face.

I had no idea if he was dying or unconscious. All I know is, his eyes were closed and he was breathing slow. I felt the car come to a stop and the officer jumped out, took him from me and ran inside. Nurses came out and rushed him to the back. That's all I remember before hitting the ground my damn self.

****

"Are you ok honey?" My father asked rubbing my hair. I glanced around the room and my mom, and Nika were staring at me.

"Oh my God. Where's Kingston?" Nika jumped up and came over to me.

"Dashier has him. What the fuck happened? You were supposed to keep him away from Dash." She did mention it to me after the DNA tests were revealed but she also said, its because Dash was a bad person and would harm Kingston. After speaking to him, I realized my cousin lied again to save face about not disclosing who my cousins father really was.

WHAP! She smacked fire from my ass. If I could've gotten up and beat her ass, I would've. The machines started beeping and I could feel the blood pressure cuff squeezing my arm.

"Bitch are you crazy slapping me?" I tried to get off the bed but my father made me stay put.

55

WHAP! My mom snacked her ass and dared her to try something. Nika's head spun to the other side and I smiled. I may not have been able to get her but my mom did.

"All you had to do is keep him at the house and I would've been there to take him." My father asked me to remain quiet, while my mother told her to leave. I have no doubt she'll return after they step out and this time, I'll make sure none of these monitors are on and beat her ass.

Ten minutes after Nika bounce, this man stepped in and I almost came on myself by how beautiful he was. Handsome didn't seem to fit how gorgeous he was. Whoever he was had to stand at least six foot two or higher. His muscles were protruding out the T-shirt, his swag was on point and so was his fresh haircut. He had diamonds in his ear and the Rolex blinded me too. I can't even explain how bad I wanted to jump his bones.

"Hello, Genesis." My eyes grew wide when I heard his voice.

There's no way this is Dashier Davis? I mean we facetimed a few times but that phone shit did him no justice.

He was a tad bit lighter, his hood persona is definitely different from the CFO bank attire I saw him in and he didn't wear all those diamonds when we spoke.

"Can you excuse us for a moment?" He asked. My mom had the biggest smile on her face and my dad, looked him up and down. I had to laugh because my dad is fat and ain't beating nobody's ass.

Once my parents stepped out, he came closer and the scent from his cologne invaded my nostrils.

"How are you?" He sat next me.

"Ok, considering." He touched the top of my nose and I winced out in pain. It couldn't be broken because I didn't have a brace on.

"How long has he been hitting you?"

"Honestly, that was the first time." He gave me a crazy look.

"I'm serious. The verbal abuse is all he ever did but it seems like he lost it when he realized I was coming to Jersey." I let my hand rest on his forearm.

"Dashier, he loves Kingston and would've never hurt him." I saw him frown.

"By no means am I saying you shouldn't have beat his ass. He deserved whatever you gave him. All I'm saying is, he's upset to see him go. Me and his family tried to make him understand but he wasn't tryna hear it."

"Did Kingston ever call him dad or pops?"

"Never. I wouldn't allow it." His smile returned.

"Dashier, I know we spoke about it on the phone but let me remind you. I had pictures of Nika and let him know every day she was indeed his mother. Did he call me mommy on a few occasions? Absolutely and I corrected him every time. Not once did he ever call Manny his father." I sat up a little more.

"Whether my cousin gave me the information or not, I knew his father would eventually come looking for him and I never wanted to confuse him." He moved a few pieces of hair out my face and I don't know why but my ass surely blushed.

"Thank you again for taking good care of him. I don't know what I would've done had he been lost in the system or went to someone who did him wrong."

"I'd do it again if I had to. Where is he?"

"He's safe. He had a concussion from that punk nigga making him hit his head. His lip was busted and he suffered a broken arm, but otherwise he's good. Do you know he asked, if I'd get him a new Nintendo switch because the other one is at the house and he never wants to go back?" I laughed. My dad got him that a few months ago just because and he loved that thing.

"Lucky for you, it's not sold out like it was when it first came out. Therefore; he'll have a lot to choose from." He tossed his head back laughing.

"What you talking about? He had me go get them in different colors. Talking about he wanted to switch up." We both shared a laugh.

"Ms. Rogers, are you ready to be discharged?" I stared at the nurse unplug my machines and moved the covers for me to stand.

"Discharged?"

"Yes. All the tests came back negative. Your nose isn't broken and you had a slight concussion. You are free to go." Her and Dash assisted me in standing.

"Hurry up and get dressed. Our flight leaves in two hours and traffic is hectic." I turned to look at him and he was paying more attention to his phone.

"You still want me to come?" He lifted his head.

"Ugh yea. You have to teach me everything he likes, as far as food, games, and other things. You have a whole month in Jersey so we need to get started."

"Ok then." I went in the bathroom to get cleaned up. A half hour later, we were leaving the hospital and on our way to the airport. It wasn't until we got there, did I see Kingston. He ran straight to me and showed me the game system his dad brought and talked about all the stuff they were gonna do. I loved this little boy and I am honestly happy he met his father.

After going through security, getting on the plane and sitting; I stared out the window and thought about all the upcoming possibilities Jersey held for me. I couldn't wait to start over.

Shanika

I told this stupid bitch to keep my son away from Dash and what does she do? Let him come take Kingston. Of course, I was gonna bounce and use him to get money outta Dashier. All the money he and his family have, a few million won't hurt any of their pockets.

If you're wondering, I absolutely knew who Dashier Davis was. Hell, you couldn't live in Jersey and not know the name. His father owned mad banks and planned on opening more. Everyone was aware Dashier would be the only one capable of taking over the empire whenever his evil ass father kicked the bucket.

I couldn't stand his parents; mainly the father. He always assumed I was a bad apple and looking for a come up. So what if he were right. His ass didn't know that in the beginning. It's not as if I walked in with a, *I'm gonna rob your son and banks* sign on my forehead.

I admit it took some years for me to get in good with Dashier because he wasn't very trusting but I did it.

Anyway, everything was going great until I met Darrell. Now the way we met, is strictly coincidental. He wasn't the mastermind behind anything because he could barely read or write. The only reason I stayed with him is because he can fuck me good and wasn't scared to use a gun.

I'm the one who coerced him into robbing banks. He wasn't with it and backed out a few times but after robbing the first one and not getting caught, he had no problem joining forces with me to do more.

We wore all black, kept our faces covered with those purge masks and even had gloves on to make sure no fingerprints were left. Unfortunately, we still got caught.

The night we were arrested, I knew it would take some time for me to be released from jail, which is why I waited patiently. I avoided any and all fights and even snitched a few times about women smuggling drugs inside, just to make it seem like I was cooperating and staying outta trouble.

Darrell and I couldn't speak or write one another in jail, because you can't interact with other inmates. He became so worried about me, he sent his mom to visit and I put on my pitiful sad face. I'm telling you, I was crying real tears about missing my son. I told her he was in a different state and cried for me everyday, blah, blah, blah. Well guess what? She went and told him and since his pussy whipped ass will do anything for me, it's exactly how I got a get out of jail free card.

He wrote a letter to the judge explaining how it was his idea and he made me do it and wallah. The judge took her own pity on me and gave me five years parole. It's basically the rest of my sentence but at least, I'm free. The only problem is, my son is in his father's care and it will be hella hard for me to take him. My dumb ass assumed bringing up the situation with Rakim would help but once he hit me with the 99.99999% I knew I lost that battle.

In any event, Rakim was correct about our situation not being what it seemed but who cares. Dash was livid and it showed on his face, and when they fought. I thought I'd die when he kicked me in the stomach. The force he used was powerful. I spit up a little blood and everything. I expected him to do more and since he didn't, I can only assume he still had love for me. However, the shit with his brother will forever bother him and to be honest, it wasn't that serious.

A year before I was arrested, I was at a party. Dash was outta town as usual and I needed a drink. My friend asked me to join her at some party this guy was throwing because she heard big ballers would be there and she wanted one. I have no idea why women threw themselves at men who made drug or some sort of illegal money, when there's plenty of rich men to have legally.

Low and behold we get to the party and it was packed. Men were definitely dripping in money and women were lusting like crazy. Half of the chicks were barely dressed and the ones that were, stood around with frowns on their faces, judging the others.

Throughout the night, I started getting fucked up and that's because my friend gave me a ecstasy pill to relax. I was worried about someone seeing me and telling Dash, who had no idea I was even here. The pill had me in a zone, horny and ready to fuck.

Somehow, I managed to make my way to the bathroom and after going, I shut the light off and it was dark as shit in the room. I didn't care because now my head was spinning and I wanted to lie down. I bumped into the bed and fell onto it, without even thinking about it and   someone else was there. I felt the person's face and it was for sure a guy who must've passed out himself.

Me, still feeling horny, didn't think twice about going down on this guy. I know its nasty and I shouldn't have but that pill and liquor mixed together had my body feeling like it was in heat. The guys' dick began to grown and I must say, I was impressed and continued sucking as if he were Dash. His hand was on top of my head and he began fucking my face. I let my own hands began to finger me at the same time.

After a few minutes of sucking, I couldn't hold out any longer and hopped on for a ride. I let my hands touch his chest and he let his guide me the way he wanted. I guess his conscious kicked in because he tossed me off him and jumped up. I tried to get back over to him but again, it was pitch black in there. Imagine both of our surprise when he flicked the light on. Shock and anger was written on Rakim's face.

"Bitch, wait til I tell my brother you out here giving head and fucking unknown niggas." I laughed and laid back in the bed watching him run and clean himself off in the bathroom.

"Oh, you're gonna tell him you fucked his girl?" I walked in and saw his hand run down his face.

"What the fuck is wrong with you?"

"You act like it wasn't a problem."

"Bitch, I thought you were Ranisha."

"Ranisha?" I questioned angrily because it meant he thought of someone else as he fucked me.

"Yea Ranisha. That's who I came with and you know it. How the hell you screwing niggas with no condoms?"

"Dash ain't here and I took an ecstasy pill. I'm so sorry Rakim." I put on my crying act and I thought he fell for it until he snatched me up by the throat.

"The only reason I'm not mentioning this to my brother is because he loves your whorish ass but make no mistake bitch.

67

I will kill you if you ever mention this." I nodded my head to let

him know I wouldn't say a word.

"Get the fuck out my face." He pushed me away and I

ran into the door. That was the last time, he and I ever spoke.

Whenever there were family functions. He'd avoid me

at all cost. He also had no problem threatening me any chance

he could. However, I knew myself the secret would come out

one day because like I said, I had plans for Dashier Davis. Did

I love him? I sure did but I was never in love and there's a

difference. The good thing about this is, he's gonna make me a

very rich woman whether he wanted to or not.

"Don't bring your ass around me again Nika." Genesis

had the nerve to shout.

"Bitch, I won't."

"Bitch? You'll call me out my name after I cared for

your son all these years? You are still ungrateful now, as you

were when we were younger."

"That's right and don't you forget it. Oh." I turned

around before stepping out the hospital room.

"If you even think about sleeping with my son's father, I'll make you regret it for the rest of your life."

"Lucky for you, I don't sleep with my cousin's men or even exs." That was a low blow because when we were in the middle school, I think it was eight grade and she liked this boy who every girl wanted. He liked her too and I interjected a few letters from him to her and he definitely had strong feelings for her, but the most they did was kiss.

Not too long after finding out, I brought him home and sucked him off. After that, he wanted nothing to do with Genesis. I think she loved him but I wanted him too and got him. Hell, we ended up being each other's first and taught one another everything in the bedroom. Yup, young as hell and I was fucking.

"He was a good fuck too Genesis. You missed out."

"Get your trifling ass outta here." My aunt yelled and my uncle shook his head in disgust. I don't care. They knew how I was and because she had my son all these years don't change a thing.

Of course, I was happy he didn't get lost in the system but that was for my own selfish reasons. At this point, it no longer matters. I'm taking Dash for everything and I may even give him some pussy one last time. Lord knows he enjoyed the way I fucked him too.

Jose

"Yo, What the fuck you doing here and get that gun out her face." I pushed Dutchess back and dared her to try something.

She is my ex, from some years back I had to leave alone because she became one of them. One of them; meaning a cop. Not only that, she was ghetto as fuck and even though I love crazy, she never knew when to turn her craziness off.

We were together fresh outta high school and it lasted two years because like I said, her dream was always to become a cop and eventually a detective. Me, being in the streets didn't think it was a good idea and ended the relationship. It was a conflict of interest at the time due to the occupation I had. She wasn't happy and it took a while for me to get rid of her but I did. Dutchess knew, just like I did that wasn't the only reason we had to part ways.

She was gorgeous, gave the best head I ever had and sex, until I met Mari. We had lots of fun together and had she not been bat shit crazy, I may have at least still fucked her but I couldn't. I felt like each time I stuck my dick in her, she

71

became even more crazy. You know how women claims a man beats on her, well it's total opposite in this case.

I couldn't speak to no chicks or she'd beat the shit outta them. She tried to fight some of the guys sister, I hung out with if they came around. If I went to the store, she had to go. I'm telling you, I can't even begin to tell you how bad it was.

"I told her to stay away from you." I felt Mari squeeze my hands.

"You sent her those messages?"

"Yup and I meant..." I didn't have a chance to react before Mari hooked off on Dutchess. The minute her goons tried to intervene, I was on it. Being I never got undressed, my weapon was still on me.

I took it out my waist and pointed it at Dutchess head, as Mari continued to bang her face on the truck. My girl had her nose and mouth bleeding. I don't think my ex expected it but that's what her ass gets. You don't show up at my place, popping shit and think it's all good. Especially; when you have no idea who you fucking with.

"Ok Mari. She gets it." I pulled her off still swinging, pushed her against my truck and lifted her face.

"It's me babe. Calm down." I pecked her lips a few times and her body began relaxing.

"You good?" She nodded and I kept my body in front of hers. Dutchess was holding her mouth and nose.

"Arrest her." She pointed and again, my weapon went up.

"I wish the fuck you would."

"She assaulted an officer."

"An officer who showed up at her man's house." Dutchess rolled her eyes.

"Yea, I'm her man. Then, you're outta uniform and putting a gun in her face over a nigga who don't want you. I think the captain will have a real good time listening to this story." I felt Mari's hands wrap around my waist. I think it was to keep me from moving forward because I took a step.

"Really Jose?" She had the nerve to ask. I ain't seen her in years and she returned assuming shit is good. Yea, she still crazy.

"Really? Fuck with my girl again and you'll be dealing with me." She backed up and into the truck.

"We have unfinished business."

"No, we don't. We've been done for years."

"Says the man who still has a soft spot for me." She smirked and had the driver peel off. I turned to see Mari staring at me.

"You still have a soft spot for her?"

"Damn, you sexy when beating a bitch ass." It made her laugh. I could tell she wanted answers but I wasn't ready to speak on it.

"Let's go inside." I lifted her up and allowed her legs to wrap around me.

"You know my dick hard." Her head rested on my shoulder.

"I didn't come over for sex but now that you mentioned it, I do wanna taste." Her hand slid in my jeans.

I closed the door behind us, let her down and tried to tear her clothes off. I had her shirt over her head, unbuttoned her jeans, pulled my dick out as she stepped out her panties and forcefully entered her.

"I swear you have the warmest, tightest and best pussy I've ever had and tasted." Our lips crashed together and the two of us were in our own world.

"You never told me that." I stopped and turned around to see Talia standing there. The bitch was still naked. This entire time, I forgot she was here.

I put Mari down and blocked her body from Talia. She seen my dick plenty of times so it doesn't matter but Mari's body is off limits to everyone but me. Granted, we were careless as fuck at the moment but who cares? This is my house and the bitch should've left when Dutchess did.

"I'ma tear that pussy up when I get in the room but I'm tasting her first." I whispered in Mari's ear and told her to wait for me in the bedroom.

"And I'm sucking all those babies out, just the way you like." She bit down on her lip and that was it.

I grabbed Talia by the arm, threw her out my house still naked and slammed the door in her face. But not before snatching the phone out her hand. I didn't know she was there, so I wasn't taking any chances that she recorded us.

****

"Damn, I make you toss bitches out and threaten them?" I put the locks on the door and watched her ass jiggle on the way up the stairs. I sure hope my sister doesn't come out the room because she's gonna see a lot.

"You make me do a lot more than that." I followed and slammed the door. I tossed Talia's phone on the dresser and reminded myself to go through it before trashing it.

"Oh yea." She fell back on the bed and tried scooting away. I grabbed both ankles and slid her to the edge. I placed my face in front of hers.

"I will kill anyone over you Mari and that's some real shit." She had both of her hands on the side of my face.

"I'm not a killer Jose but you already know I'm beating a bitch ass over you and if she dies by me doing it, then so be it."

"We may as well get married then." I joked and she smiled.

"Why not? I'm married to this dick." She moved closer so the tip touched her entrance.

"And I'm married to this banging ass pussy that's for damn sure. Matter of fact, let me eat it."

"Make me scream daddy." My dick twitched when she said it. I loved hearing her moan out my name.

After making her yell out that she couldn't take anymore, I stood and entered her most treasured place. I lifted her legs and buried my dick deep inside, until her pussy was on the root of it.

I could feel her grinding under me, let her legs down and placed them in the crook of my arms. It felt good as hell and the sounds of our skin smacking and watching our juices flowing, enhanced the pleasure to a whole other level.

I wrapped her legs around my waist and stood with our bodies still connected, only to force her against the wall and place her hands above her head. I loved watching her squirm and moan in this position. Something about the way she dug her nails in my shoulders each time I thrusted harder, put me in a different frame of mind. I would always go deeper, to make her orgasm stronger than the previous one.

"Joseeeeeee. Baby, it feels goooooood." Her hands were tangled in my hair and the way her body shook, was mesmerizing.

"Nobody will ever have your body cumming like this." I let my teeth scrape down the side of her neck, making goosebumps pop up on her arms and legs.

I placed her on all fours and watched her ass jiggle each time I hammered in and out. I began feeling the pull on my dick, urging me to cum, increased my pumping and made her cry out as her hands gripped the blanket.

"Oh God Jose. Shit." She made every attempt to stifle those moans and cries but it was no use. Her body was consumed by immense satisfaction making her almost collapsed on the bed. My hands went under her stomach, lifted her up and grabbed her waist.

My body began fighting a battle of its own again. Every part was aching for my balls to release all this cum. I had to hurry up and this time, I'm not telling her to suck me off. I'm staking claim on her and since we already decided no one can have the other, I may as well give her my seeds.

"Baby, I can't hold out any longer." I whispered outta breath in her ear as my chest touched her back. I let my hand slide in her hair, grasped at it tightly, bit down on her shoulder, and shot loads of cum inside her. Even if I wanted to pull out, I couldn't because it felt too damn good.

I lowered her body on the bed and fell on the side of her. Both of us were weak. Her juices covered my dick and it glistened in the moonlight coming from the window. I ain't even gonna front. I pray she gets pregnant. At least, I know she won't be with anyone else.

"You good?" I smacked her ass under the covers.

"As long as you got me, I am." I turned her body to mine.

"One thing you'll never have to worry about is me cheating."

"Jose, I didn't…" I used my finger to keep her from speaking.

"I know my ex showing up, sending those stupid ass messages, tryna fight you and saying I have a soft spot for her may have you thinking differently."

"Tryna fight? I don't think so. I beat that ass." I started cracking up.

"You did but don't let her words bother you." I gave her eye to eye contact so she could tell how serious I was.

"Demaris Davis is the only woman I wanna be with."

"I better be or I'll..." I let my lips press against hers.

"Don't let how nice I am to you, get yo ass beat." She had a crazy look on her face.

"Goodnight and fix your face." I turned over and pulled the covers up. She moved closer to me, letting her breasts touch my back and her arms went around my waist. I pulled her hand up and kissed it. I swear this woman had me gone. I couldn't get away from her, even if I wanted to.

Demaris

"Mmmm. Morning baby." I said quietly with the covers over my mouth. Jose was placing kisses on my neck and shoulder.

"Morning. You hungry?"

"You cooking?" He turned my body to face him.

"Nah, Jocelyn is woke and I smell food."

"It may only be for you." I didn't know if his sister knew I stayed the night and only cooked for them.

"Even if she did, you can have it." I smiled and thought about Jennifer Lewis in the movie Brothers. She said, if a man gives you his last, it means he loves you.

"Why you smiling?" I shrugged my shoulders, removed the covers and went in his private bathroom. He came in and passed me, my toothbrush and mouthwash. Yup! I have stuff here too so even if a bitch did come by, she'd know all about me.

"You love me Jose?" I spit the toothpaste out and began brushing again. He lifted my face and made my eyes meet his in the mirror.

"I didn't know for sure how I felt until she had the gun in your face." I spit again, rinsed my mouth and turned around.

"One simple mistake and your life could've been snatched away. Mari." He stared into my eyes again but this time I felt like he could see straight through me.

"If anything would've happened to you, I can't say all of them wouldn't have died too, especially; her. The thought of you never waking up to me, letting me make love to you or even being in your presence had a nigga losing it."

"Jose, I..." he cut me off.

"I'm deep in love with you Mari and I'ma do my best to keep you safe at all times." I tried to speak again and he shut me down.

"The only reason she got to you is because I had no idea her ass came to town."

"How is that possible?" He picked his toothbrush up and began doing the same as me. He spit a few times, wiped his face and looked at me.

"She's been away for years, and I wanna apologize for snapping on you the day you sent the photo. I just knew no one from my past did it but it turned out, it's exactly who did, which is why I'm gonna kill her." He kissed me gently, picked the mouthwash up and began gargling. I said nothing and went to start the shower. He claimed he'll kill for me and if she's where he has to start, oh well.

"Come here daddy." He turned and smiled. I knew how much he loved me calling him that.

"I need some for the road." I gestured for him to join me.

"Is that right?" He stepped in and closed the glass door.

"It's exactly right and I'm in love with you too." I leaped in his arms and he slid down on the bench.

"God, what is it about you that gets me so got damn horny and wet?" I moaned and aggressively began kissing him.

He fisted my hair, pulled it back and sucked on my neck, as he sheathed himself inside me. He cupped both of my ass cheeks, spread them open and slid his finger in my ass. This is the first time he tried it and the feeling was amazing. I don't know if I was having an outer body experience or what.

All I know is, it felt incredible letting go and being taken by him.

"Fuck me Mari."

Jose began lifting me up and dropping my lower half harder on top of him. I intertwined my hands in his, rested them above his head like he does me and rode him like a wild stallion. I could feel him deeper with each thrust. My hips were bucking, eyes rolled and once his dick twitched, I knew it was time for both of us to release.

We were moaning each other's name loud and didn't care who heard us. I went faster, dropped harder, grinded in circles and within minutes, I screamed out as both of us relieved ourselves in one another. My head fell on his chest and I was ready to close my eyes.

"That was intense." I said breathlessly as he moved the strands of hair out my face.

"You really fucked the shit outta me."

"I'm always gonna make that my mission. Can we eat now?" He laughed and grabbed the soap and rag to wash us up.

"Oh and I got questions." He busted out laughing. I'm sure he knew I'd say something sooner or later. Ain't no way in hell we bypassing the shit with his ex.

****

"Smells good sis. What you make?" Jose let my hand go and went to the stove.

"Ugh, I made me and Mari something to eat. You're gonna have to make your own." She squeezed his cheek.

"How you know she even wants your food? You know she thinks you let Talia in to fuck me." I smacked him on the arm.

"What? You did." He opened the refrigerator and grabbed the orange juice, then went in the cabinet to grab glasses.

"I know how Jose feels about you Mari. Some sisters may cover for their brother but that's not me. If his ass had another chick in here and I knew, I would've called you."

"Thank you Jocelyn and I apologize for thinking you did. She came to the door naked and…"

85

"And you thought she got some of this good ass dick, that curves and make you cum a lot; didn't you?" He grabbed me from behind and kissed my neck.

"I can't stand you."

"That's not what you were just saying when…"

"It's too early Jose." She started speaking in Spanish and when he responded, my pussy got a little moist.

I hear him whisper in Spanish when we're having sex, but I've never heard him have an actual conversation in it. He sounded sexy as hell and he knew because his nasty ass smirked and rolled his tongue.

"The weirdest things turn you on."

"Whatever." He sat next to me and I fed him some eggs off my plate. Jocelyn really didn't make him any food.

"I may as well had made him some since you're giving it all to him."

"She's not gonna see her man starve. Anyway, I'm about to be an uncle and since you're gonna marry me, you'll be an aunt."

"Really!" I hopped out the chair and rubbed her stomach. She gave Jose the evilest look and I backed up.

"I'm sorry if I overstepped."

"It's not you she's mad at Mari. It's me and the nigga."

"Don't tell me he doesn't want the baby." Jocelyn slammed her plate down and plopped in the chair. Her hands ran through that long mane of hers and she stared at the ceiling.

"I recently found out about the pregnancy and couldn't even be excited because his dirty ass was still fucking this other chick. Evidently, she gave him Trich and now I have it, well had it. I want the baby but it's gonna make him stay in my life for the next eighteen years and I don't want that."

"Let me guess. The guy said, you better not get rid of it, regardless of him giving you something and tried to stop you from leaving." She nodded her head yes and wiped the few tears falling.

"How the hell would you know? I popped that cherry and ain't no other nigga been in it. Sooooooo, how you become an expert?" I rolled my eyes at him.

"First of all, it's the same with all men when they cheat on a woman. They expect them to forgive, forget and move on when it's not as easy for women, as it is for men. And second… who said I wanted Jocelyn to know you were my first?" He took a piece of bacon off my plate and made me eat it.

"She don't care and you need to feed the child I put in you last night." I started choking hard as hell. My eyes were watering, and I could barely catch my breath. He thought the shit was hysterical, while Jocelyn hopped up, had me put my hands up and patted me on the back.

"Don't act like you didn't know, I shot your club up. A couple times, I may add." I took a sip of orange juice and slammed the glass down.

"Jose, we haven't even discussed anything."

"Yes we did. Don't you remember?" I folded my arms across my chest.

"I think it went something like, *Jose, you feel so good.*"

"That does not mean get me pregnant."

"And I told you, I couldn't hold out. Not once did you say pull out, make me stop or take my kids from me in another way. Therefore; you were a willing participant." I sat there looking like a damn fool. Him and Jocelyn were both laughing at me. I picked my fork up and started eating.

"See, you already pregnant. Look how you are scarfing down those pancakes." I dropped the fork and pushed the chair out.

"Let's see how funny it is when…"

"I wish you would say it." He came towards me slowly. Jocelyn shook her head. She probably thought we were crazy.

"Say it Mari." I backed up and almost tripped over the step that led into the living room.

"You're too close. Back up." I put my hand on his chest. His entire demeanor was changing before my eyes and not in a good way.

"I was gonna say, see if it's funny if…"

"If what?-" I hit the wall.

"If we have twins." His facial expression changed back to happy and my heart started to beat again. I ain't even gonna lie. He had me scared to death. I did plan on saying what if I took a plan b but quickly changed my mind. This nigga is crazy, and I can't imagine what he'd do, if I did.

"It better be what you were gonna say."

"You can't keep threatening me. It's not going to make me stick around." His hand went in my hair.

"You're never leaving me Mari and vice versa, so stop assuming your fake ass threats are gonna scare me."

"Don't make me leave you." I pushed him away and he grabbed both of my hands.

"I won't and even if I did by doing something stupid, I'm still gonna stalk you." We both stared at each other and busted out laughing.

"I'm not gonna hurt you Mari." He kissed me feverishly and had Jocelyn not cleared her throat, we may have gotten naked right here.

"I'm going to lay down for a little while."

"That's gonna be you soon Mari. Eating and sleeping all day." He got a kick outta cumming in me, where I was scared as hell. I'm still young and have no idea what to do with a child. And he thinks, he's the only one who'd kill me if I terminated a pregnancy. Not at all. My parents would kill me, after my brothers.

"We need to discuss your little female friends showing up unannounced." He looked down at his phone and then at me.

"Where's your phone?"

"Upstairs, why?"

"Is it on?"

"Oh shit. I turned it off last night when I got here, thinking we'd be fucking at the door but you had company and…"

"Go get your stuff." His tone changed.

"Are you kicking me out?"

"Never. I got a text from your brother and he said you need to call your parents and get to the hospital." My nerves immediately went into overdrive.

"Did he say what happened?"

"No. Come on, I'll drive you. I can't have you killing my child on the way." He smacked my ass on the way up the steps.

91

"Stop saying that. You don't even know if…"

"Yes, I do. I gave you buckets of cum. There's no way one of them ain't hit the mark." I sucked my teeth, grabbed my things and headed out the door.

When I turned my phone on, I had tons of notifications. Nothing explained what happened, but every text asked where I was and to get over to the hospital. I hope everything is ok. I don't know if I could take anything happening to my brothers.

"It's gonna be fine Mari." Jose grabbed my hand and kissed the back of it. I nodded and stared at the window.

When we got there, he had to help me out because I had a bad feeling about going in. Once I called my parents and found out what floor they were on, I didn't expect to see anything like this.

Levion

I was talking to George on the phone when he
mentioned seeing Efrain. Well, he wasn't sure because they
only met the night Mari had gotten shot at my club. To this day,
we have yet to find the culprit behind that.

Anyway, George said something about him fighting,
which isn't unlike my brother at all. Efrain had a lot of anger
issues but only acted on it, if provoked. It wasn't until he spoke
of it being more than one guy hitting him, that I became
worried. I told George not to go any further, but it was too late.
I heard a noise, what sounded like the phone hitting the ground
and then the call disconnected.

I was on my way home from work and hit a detour to
go in the direction of the store. Unfortunately, when I arrived
cops were everywhere, so were the ambulances but there
wasn't anyone in police custody. Unless, another cop car
pulled off with the assailant(s), they obviously had no one.

Sad to say, I witnessed George going in the ambulance
unconscious and my brother appeared to be dead. There was a
gash across his neck, but it wasn't from a knife. His head and

face had blood covering it and one of his legs had to be dislocated by the way it looked. I called my parents up right away and told them to meet me at the hospital.

No one seemed to know what happened because where it took place at was away from the store, however; when I turned to survey the parking lot, I noticed two cameras facing other areas. There was also one across the street.

As soon as George gets well, I'm gonna be all over it. I could've done it already, but he didn't want me to leave. I only hope the cops don't mess up the footage before I can see it. For no one to see a thing, I can only assume the person has some sort of affiliation with them.

George suffered a seizure due to the object hitting him in the back of his head. The doctor said, he may suffer memory loss, here and there. He also has a bruised neck from the fall. He had on a neck brace but took it off when they told him it was only a bruise. I had to laugh because I probably would've done the same exact thing.

I wanted my siblings here but after hearing the shit with Rakim and Dash, I knew they couldn't be in the same room together. Efrain is in ICU, in a coma and no one has heard from Mari. I've been calling her all night.

To make matters worse, Dash called and told us what went down in Alabama with his son and some guy. It seemed like our family was being hit from every angle.

"Oh my God son. Are you ok?" George's mom moved straight passed me without speaking. Not that I care because his parents don't agree with his lifestyle and accuse every person he's been with, the person who turned him. She even had the nerve to say I threatened him to be this way.

"Hello mother. What are you doing here?" If you can't tell, George isn't beat for his mother or family either. His sister is the only one who doesn't seem bothered by him being gay and I think it's because her ass dipped a few times.

"I'm fine and why are you here?"

"Son, don't speak to your mother that way." His father said and he sucked his teeth. He's one of the old-fashioned men who was set in his ways. The sad part is he worked in the court system, so imagine how many people he probably fucked over.

"I'll be outside."

"You don't have to go Levi." George said it in a way that let me know he wanted me to stay.

He only speaks to his family on the holidays and even then, he ends up coming home early due to their ignorance. I can't even tell you how they knew he was here because he begged me not to inform them. If I were a parent, I'd want someone to contact me but everyone is different.

"Yes, he does. He shouldn't have even been here before us."

"Ma, don't start your shit. He is my man and has every right to be here." She sucked her teeth.

"Honey, that knot on your head didn't bring you outta this gay phase? I mean, it's been a long time now and you've experienced enough."

"It's best for me to stand outside."

"Levi, no." He stared at his father and for some reason, shit didn't sit right with me. It's like he was scared or something.

96

"I'll be right outside the door and if anyone and I mean anyone, touches a single hair on you, I'm knocking them the fuck out." I looked his father up and down.

George smiled and seemed a bit more relaxed hearing me threaten his parents. Yea, some shit goes down at their house and he's gonna tell me when they leave.

"Levion what happened?" Mari came running towards me with tears coming down her face. I had to take a double look because there's no way this is the guy she's messing with.

"George and Efrain got hurt and what are you doing with him? What up Jose?" He spoke and Mari turned from me to him.

"You two know one another?" She wiped her eyes.

"Yea, he does my books. Dashier sent him my way a while back. The question is, what are you doing with him and how do you know him?" I stared down at her blushing.

"Well, he… Ugh, we… The two of us met… And yea we're…" I laughed at her stuttering and fidgeting with her fingers.

"She's my woman and Mari, why you acting ashamed of me?" She snapped her neck to stare at him.

"I'm not Jose and don't you start with me."

"I'm just saying, most women will say, he's my man but you're hesitating." She stuck her tongue at him and grabbed his hand.

"This is my soon to be ex if he don't stop playing."

"Stop lying to yourself. I told you before we ain't ever breaking up. Anyway, how's George?" I got a kick outta them already.

"He's good right now. I'm waiting to hear about Efrain."

"What all went down and did they find the person or people who did it?"

"No and.-" I was about to answer when I heard something that sounded like glass crash in George's room. We all went in and his father had his hands around his throat. My first reaction was to murk him right there but instead, I wrapped my arm around his neck and put his ass to sleep.

"Oh dear God. What did you do?" Mari ran over to check on George while Jose did his best holding me back.

"Bitch, don't ask me what I did when you stood right there allowing him to choke my man. Tha fuck wrong with you?" I guess she thought I'd be some flamboyant gay man but she was wrong. The nigga came right out when I saw the shit her husband did.

"How dare you?"

"How dare I what? Protect him from a motherfucker like him?" I pointed on the ground. I pressed the button to the nurse's station and asked her to bring security in this room. I stepped in his mother's face.

"From this day forward, don't call or bring your ass around him."

"I'm his mother."

"I don't give a fuck. If I catch you or any of your family around him, I'm going to do a lot worse. Don't fuck with me bitch." She backed herself into the wall.

"Is everything ok in here?" Two security dudes ran in.

"Actually, it's not. This man tried to kill me." George spoke up and his mother was shocked to say the least. One of the security dudes made a phone call and had someone contact the police.

After about an hour of having the cops get his statements, his mother crying, saying I threatened her and watching his father get carted off to jail, shit was back to normal.

Mari, stayed the entire time to keep me calm because I wanted to beat the shit outta his mom for popping mad shit. Even Jose, had to step in and get me to stand outside the door.

"Thank you so much babe. You have no idea how long I've been waiting to tell on him." I gave him a crazy look.

"I wanted to tell you but I didn't need you in jail. I mean, who would I lay next to at night and.-" He stopped and smirked.

"No one because then I'd have to kill you." I laid in bed with him and pecked his lips. He definitely had an effect on me, which is why a peck is all he got even though he wanted more.

He won't have my ass moaning in this damn hospital. Homothug or not, some shit needs to remain private.

****

"I'll be back in a few. Mari is here if you need anything." I told George who just came home. They made him stay two days for observation. The doctor asked not to leave him alone for a week.

"But I wanna…" I cut him off.

"I know what you want and I'll handle it when I get home. You make sure you're ready." He smiled and blew me a kiss.

"How's he doing?" Mari questioned as soon as I hit the kitchen.

"Better. How's Efrain?" She and I were gonna take turns sitting with him.

"Still no change. Mommy has been up there and daddy is calling everyday." I nodded. My father was doing better but the doctor had him on bedrest for a little longer. He went to the hospital the day Efrain was attacked but he's been home ever

101

since. I know it's killing him because Efrain is the baby outta the boys.

"A'ight. I'll be home in a few hours."

"Is it ok if Jose stops by?" I stared at her and the smile gracing her face is all I needed to see, to know she's in love.

"Let me find out he done strung your virgin ass out." Her mouth fell open.

"You know damn well George tells me everything."

"I ain't telling him shit else. He talks too much." I was cracking up.

"He didn't tell me a lot."

"What did he tell you?"

"That you found your dream guy and he helped you prepare for the first time."

"Anyway, he and I are exploring one another and…"

"Sis, who you talking too? That nigga fucking the shit outta you and I guarantee you'll be pregnant soon because like he said, *you ain't ever leaving him.*" I put in air quotes and she threw the entire roll of paper towels at me.

"GET OUT!"

"How you kicking me out my own shit?"

"Because I can. GO!" She pointed to the door at the same time it rang. I glanced over at her and she waved me off. I opened the door and what do you know.

"Hey Jose. I didn't know you were stopping by."

"Mari, I told you to mention it. I don't like showing up at people's house and they don't know."

"Oh, she said someone was coming through. I asked was it you and she said no. Sooooo, I think you better check that shit."

"Oh my God Levi, why you lying?" She screamed and Jose ice grilled the hell outta her.

"Do me a favor and have that rough sex at your own house later."

"It's definitely on when we leave." Mari was hot to death, where I was cracking the hell up. That's what her ass gets for tryna be funny.

I'm no fool when it comes to my sister being in love and I see it all over her face as well as his. Plus, Dash told me not too long ago that Jose was strung out too. The crazy part is, they were or should I say she, was hiding him like we would be

mad she had a man. I'm happy she found someone to love her

the right way because that nigga Ethan didn't.

Rakim

"Ok sir. All you test results came back negative and the HIV is non-reactive." The doctor told me. Hell yea, I ran to him the day after all the shit kicked off at my house with lying ass Nika, disease giving Ranisha and pissed off Jocelyn.

"What the hell does non-reactive mean?" I was confused.

"If the rest say negative, why doesn't the HIV test say it too?"

"It's the way the results are completed but you are negative. Also, you and your partner should return to take another one in six months."

"For what?"

"If you recently had unprotected sex, it may not have run through your system. Studies suggest it takes up to 12 weeks, therefore; they'll get a better answer after that time." I snatched the paper out his hand.

"Is this HIV test negative?"

"Well yes but..."

"But my ass. Y'all doctors always tryna scare motherfuckers by telling them to take another one. Why in the hell would I take another one and this is negative? It's like a woman taking a pregnancy test. You're not going to give her blood work and make her re-do another one to make sure she's pregnant. Fuck outta here with that."

"Mr. Davis, I understand your frustration, however; it's my job to tell you."

"Well you told me I'm negative and that's the only thing that matters. Moving on." I folded the paper up and put it in my pocket.

"My girl just found out she's pregnant. How long before a termination is no longer an option?" I had my arms folded waiting to hear.

"Depending on how far she is now, most facilities only perform abortions up to 16-20 weeks. Some may do it further along but it's not recommended. Mr. Davis, I have to ask. Did she?-" I cut him off.

"Yes, she's been tested. It's how I found out about the Trich shit." He nodded. I'm positive Jocelyn took her ass back

106

to the doctor and had those tests done. I also knew if I gave her anything else, she definitely wouldn't hesitate to let me know.

"Do you have any more questions Mr. Davis?"

"No. I'll see you later." I hit him with the peace sign and left.

As I drove out the doctor's office, I thought about the things that transpired. I got a disease by some bitch who clearly gets it all the time. Had my brother's ex claim my nephew is my son, which I knew was false off the bat. And lost Jocelyn.

She won't take any of my calls and yesterday had the nerve to change her got damn number. It's all good because once my family is back on track, I'll see about her too.

I'm also tryna find out who attacked my brother and George. Efrain has a bad attitude but he doesn't bother anyone unless pushed. And poor George. From what Levi explained to me, he was tryna see if he were ok and got caught up as well.

Some think Levion is quiet but that nigga just as crazy as the rest of us. When he called to tell me what happened, not only did he cry about our brother but George too. I knew right then he really did love dude.

I'm not homophobic at all, but I didn't want a gay man in my family or as my brother. However; Levi loves who he loves and I'm not gonna stop speaking or loving him because of it. I'm fine with my sexuality so it doesn't bother me at all. I will always feel like, as long as George doesn't hurt him, we good. It doesn't matter who a person is with, they can break your heart just the same. It's funny because no one has a problem when two women are together, especially; if they're bad but let it be two men and the world is over.

****

I parked in front of my office, stepped out and went inside to meet with Cedric and the team. My brother had been laid up in a coma and we had no leads, which is unacceptable because someone, saw something.

"They all here Boss." Ced opened the conference room door and the entire team was in there; including their workers. I wanted everyone in attendance to hear what I had to say.

"Time is money so I'm gonna be fast to let you back on the streets doing what you do best." I walked to the front of the

108

table and like always, stared each individual down. Nothing or no one struck me as suspicious.

"As you may or may not know, my brother was attacked outside of a store. The person who asked, if he needed assistance, suffered an attack as well." I noticed a few dudes shaking their heads.

I didn't mention George's name or how he's affiliated with my family. Levi hasn't told anyone about their relationship as far as I knew and I didn't want to tell his business.

"Long story short, no one claims to know anything but I'm offering a 250k award to anyone who comes forward with the information." You heard a lotta gasping and people saying, got damn that's a lot of money but no one spoke up.

"You know snitching don't run in my blood so whoever reveals the story won't have to worry about retaliation coming from anyone." Everyone nodded.

"Even if none of you know, put your ears to the street and I don't care if someone describes the sneakers the person wore who did it, it's a start. Each piece of information will also

109

come with a reward just so you know." I wanted everyone looking in hopes to get rich. Money is the root of all evil and niggas will tell quick.

"Boss, I heard one of the dudes that did it, don't live around here." Ron, one of workers shouted. The entire room stared at him.

"Who told you that?" I walked over to where he sat.

"I sent a message to my brother. He hears a lot at the club he works at."

"Did he say who?" I glanced at the message and sure enough, he overheard people discussing it at work.

"Where does he work?" When he mentioned my brother's spot, I hit Levi up and told him to go question the guy.

"Thanks, and for that small amount of info, I'm giving you 5k." I nodded to Ced who left to retrieve the money out the safe.

"Oh hell yea. I'm about to search everywhere." Another guy yelled out. The room erupted in laughter.

"I'm serious? 5k for that. Yea, I'm knocking on doors."

"You don't have to go that far but I appreciate money motivating you."

"Here you go." Ced passed the money and just as I was going to dismiss them, the look on Gavin's face was quite disturbing. He was sweating, fidgeting with his hands and appeared to be nervous. I smirked at Ced who noticed the same.

"Everyone can go except Gavin." He turned to me and asked why. Once the team left, I sat next to him and Ced sat on the other side.

"What's good Gavin?" I placed my hands on my stomach and leaned back.

"I don't know what you mean." He gave a fake smile.

"Seeing as though you're sweating like a slave and fidgeting, I'd say you have some things on your mind. What you think Ced?"

"I'd say the same. Where were you the night his brother got attacked?"

"I... was at my...." the stuttering is a dead giveaway. He's not capable of doing the things to my brother these people did but he's definitely hiding something.

"Where were you?" He put his head down and started crying like the baby he is.

"The people came up short at my father's job and I had to use my own money to pay you. I've been stressing a lot over it and..."

"And why didn't you mention it? One of us could've dealt with the situation." If I couldn't do something, Ced handled it. He is just like me when it comes to money and family, so I have no doubt we wouldn't be having this conversation if he had told him.

"I didn't wanna bother y'all. Especially; after serving your brother." I punched him in the face for GP. Thinking about my brother getting high pissed me off. Ced shook his head laughing.

"Since you figured out a way to handle shit, I expect whatever is going on at your father's job, gets fixed ASAP. Otherwise; myself or Ced here will be paying you a visit." I rose to my feet and walked out. I heard Ced hooking off and laughed. That's my nigga. We couldn't stand Gavin and we'd beat his ass for any reason at all.

Next stop is the hospital. I need to go and see Efrain. I stayed away because I didn't wanna see him laid up and I was giving Dash time to cool off. Even if we never speak again, I'm not distancing myself from my other siblings. Eventually, we'll have to be in the same room so fuck it.

Efrain

"Can you feel this Mr. Davis?" The doctor asked running that reflex thing up and down my foot. I nodded my head yes because for some reason, they had this mouth thing in and told me not to remove it yet. I don't know why. It's obvious my ass breathing on my own.

"What about this?" He ran it down the center of my chest and I nodded yes again.

"Good. No paralysis evident and he's alert." He opened my eyes to flash the light in it and then up my nose and ears.

This must be the bullshit ass exam after getting beat the fuck up. He ordered a few tests and put gloves on. As he pulled the tube out my mouth, my mother, father, and Rakim stepped in the room. The whole time I was in a coma, I heard everyone's voice except Rakim's. He better have a damn good excuse on why he hadn't been here.

Once the doctor finished he left and told them, I'll be in and out for test. He requested MRI's for my head and leg. Cat Scans and X-rays too. Don't ask me why, when I thought you could tell everything through an MRI.

114

"Are you ok?" My mom kissed my forehead and wiped her tears. My father smiled and grabbed my hand as Rakim helped him in a chair.

"I'm ok. How long have I been out?"

"A little over a month."

"Send a text out to your brothers and sister that he's awake." The look Rakim gave her had me questioning it myself. Did I miss something?

"If you don't want to text him, have Demaris or Levion do it but don't you dare leave him out."

"A'ight ma."

"Rakim." My father spoke in a firm tone and my brother apologized.

"Son, do you remember what happened?" My mom put a straw in the cup of water she poured and helped me sit up, in order to drink.

"I was arguing with a guy and he and his two friends fought me, hit me with a metal bat and used some sort of wire around my neck." I barely got the whisper out. My throat was sore as hell but I knew they wanted answers.

115

"Why on earth would they do that?" I had to answer the next question delicately because if anyone knew the person responsible, they'd kill them and I wanna do it myself; especially Bobby.

"No idea ma. Maybe they were in a bad mood the night we came in contact. Wait! Is George ok?"

"Yea. He's home with your brother. I'm so happy you woke up." She hugged me and Rakim had to pull her off. She was squeezing the hell outta me.

The three of them stayed with me for the rest of the day. I thought they'd leave when it was time to go for test but they were still there when I returned. They did leave around seven.

I loved the hell outta my family but what I'm gonna do when I get better, is going to require all of my siblings finding out and I don't think I'm ready to relive those memories.

"Efrain, we don't have to stay long. It will just be for an hour." My girl Nicole wanted to hit another one of Gavin's parties. I was over it because my grades were dropping and my parents were complaining about being out every weekend.

"This is the last one for a while Nicole." She jumped up and down like a kid in the candy store. Why the fuck is she so damn happy?

The night of the party, it was packed as usual with people from everywhere. Nicole ran into some of the chicks from high school and left me. I didn't mind and went to speak with a few guys I knew. After about two hours of being there and damn near drunk outta my mind, I stumbled in a room with a few guys inside. I had no idea who they were and backed out. I may have been drunk, but I knew better than to associate with other drunk motherfuckers I didn't know.

I found the bathroom, used it and made my way to the steps. I had to hold on to the banister because I was about to fall. My feet hit the bottom step, when I felt someone grabbing me back up. I started swinging immediately. It didn't matter though because once the person or persons had me at the top of the steps, someone grabbed my ankles and drug me in a dark room. You could see people sitting next to the small moon lamps. Music was playing and I heard a few voices asking what they were doing and why did they bring me in there.

117

"This the nigga who's fucking Nicole." One guy said.

"Ok and the bitch is a ho." That shit bothered me so I hooked off on him. We began fighting and shit went downhill from there.

"Efrain, you good?" My sister was shaking the hell outta me.

"Mari?"

"Yes, it's me. Are you ok?" Her eyes were watery and she asked someone to bring her a wet towel.

"I'm fine. Why the hell you giving me shaking baby syndrome?"

"I told her to stop shaking you like that." I heard a male voice and looked over to see the same Spanish looking dude from the diner. She sucked her teeth at him and snatched the washcloth.

"You were shaking and cursing in your sleep. Whose Bobby and is he the one who did this to you?" I stared at her asking me questions. Did I speak that much in my dream?

"No one. Who is this?" She finished wiping down my face and passed me a toothbrush, toothpaste and one of those small bed pan looking things to brush my teeth, talking about I will not speak to her with funky breath. When I finished she removed it from in front of me and came over to speak.

"Jose, this is my brother Efrain and Efrain, this is…"

"You better not hesitate either Mari."

"You didn't even let me finish, damn."

"I'm just saying. You stuttered when Levi asked."

"Awww poor baby. You still dwelling on that? Come here." He leaned down for her to whisper in his ear and I turned my head once he smiled. She must've been saying some nasty shit to him.

"Really Mari. He fucking you that good?"

"Yooooo! I know you her brother and all but don't disrespect her like that." His face turned up and Mari stepped in the middle.

"Efrain, what the hell is wrong with you? And if you must know, yes he is." Jose stared at both of us and we busted out laughing. She and I had our own way of communicating.

"Before I was rudely interrupted Efrain, this is my man Jose and he was my first."

119

"And last. Mari, stop playing with me."

"Hold up. Mari you're stuck with him for life? How the hell you supposed to experience if he's the best or not? I mean, who would you compare him too?" Dude was so fucking mad.

"I swear to God, I'ma about to murk you and her."

"Jose, you'd kill me?" She sashayed over to him on the chair and sat on his lap.

"Who would do the things to you, I do if I'm dead?"

"Get off Mari. You play too damn much." He tried to push her off.

"Fine! I guess I'm gonna go sample..." He yanked her arm and held her in front of the wall.

"I'm tryna be respectful in front of your brother but I promise when we get home, I'm gonna have you walking funny for a week."

"Alright Jose damn." She moved away.

"Now it's alright but guess what Mari? It's too late. It's on." She waved him off and sat next to me.

"Damn sis. You got him hooked already?"

"I think it's my head game." She said and I pushed her off the bed.

"We play a lot but I definitely don't wanna hear that shit."

"Both of y'all are gonna stop pushing me." She stood and walked out to find housekeeping to clean my sheets and get a soda out the vending machine. She claims the hospital sodas are flat.

"I see you got who you wanted." Jose turned to face me.

"I remember you from the diner." He squinted his eyes and smirked.

"You're the nigga who knocked Talia out."

"That's me. As you can see we play no games about Mari."

"Me either."

"Does Rakim know about y'all yet?" He ran his hand over his head and explained how Mari is nervous because he told her not to date Jose. If you ask me, I think he's perfect for her. He gets in her ass and appears to be overprotective already

121

and I've only known him for maybe ten minutes. If you can portray yourself like that in the beginning, you get my vote.

"Yo, let me ask you a question." I removed the covers off my leg, slid them over and asked him to pass me the crutches. My leg was broken in four spots and the doctor said, I'd be in a cast for at least six to eight weeks.

"What's up with her and Talia? Did they know one another prior to me?" I chuckled and asked him to open the bathroom door.

"Let Mari tell you but I will say, keep Talia away from her."

"Trust me, I've seen the damage Mari did to her and one of my ex's." I stopped and looked at him.

"Jose, I can tell how much you're feeling my sister and vice versa but as her brother, and I'm speaking for my entire family, don't have her out there fighting."

"It wasn't like that." He told me everything that happened and even though he couldn't control what went down, I told him it's still his shit and she shouldn't have to lay bitches out.

"Talia, is going to remain a problem because after the previous incident with her, she told Mari she's gonna fuck with her any chance she get. Now, Mari may not be a fighter."

"Sheiiittttt."

"I'm not saying she can't fight." We both laughed.

"I'm saying, she won't unless pushed and none of us want her out there fighting."

"I don't want her fighting either, but she's fast as hell."

"That she is."

"And I think she's pregnant and scared to find out." He shrugged and went to sit in the chair.

"SAY WHAT?" I wasn't mad at all. I was excited as hell to be honest.

"Yea, she didn't make me pull out and…"

"Bro, I'm good on the rest of that conversation."

"Anyway, it's only been a few weeks but I already see a change in her and if you don't know, women feel different during pregnancy."

"Ok, I'm done. Let me know if she is." He got a kick outta making me nauseous.

I went in the bathroom, cleaned myself up and came out feeling a lot better. My sheets were cleaned and I noticed Mari sitting on Jose's lap and him rubbing her stomach. She kept telling him to stop and it wasn't happening. I was happy and nervous for her.

My mom is going to be overjoyed and my dad will be ok with whatever Mari's ok with. However; Mari is super spoiled and I don't know how Jose is gonna deal with her and a baby being the same. Let alone, those shopping habits are gonna increase like crazy.

"Hello Efrain." Mari and Jose looked up and I sucked my teeth. The audacity of this bitch showing her face.

"GET THE FUCK OUT!" Unfortunately, Jose never lied when he said my sister was fast. She jumped on Nicole so quick, neither of us could stop her. Mari was beating the crap outta her that fast. Jose jumped up and pulled Mari off.

"You stupid bitch." Nicole yelled out and Jose damn near lost it on her. My sister had to get in front, to stop him from whooping Nicole's ass.

"I only came to see if you were ok and ask if therapy was helping."

"Bitch, he don't need no got damn therapy for you bouncing the way you did." Nicole snickered.

"I see you kept that secret to yourself huh?" The way she said it let me know she's about to try and tell what happened that night.

"Whatever secret you're speaking of, we know all about and if you even think about revealing it, I'm gonna find you and do worse than I did." The look on Nicole's face was funny. Here she thought shouting out the shit would be fun for her, but it backfired because my sister was on it.

"Don't bring your dumb ass around him again."

"Efrain, I'm sorry. If I could change the way things went down, I would." Why is she even apologizing after threatening to expose everything?

"GET OUT!" I shouted when she brought it up.

"Efrain." I reached over and tossed one of the crutches at her. It hit her in the head and then the floor. She ran off and

Mari snapped her head to look at me. Jose closed the door and she walked over to my bedside, sat down and held my hand.

"Efrain, I don't know what she's speaking of and until you're ready to discuss it, I won't ask questions. I just want you to know whatever it is, I'll be here when you wanna talk about it." She wiped the lone tear falling down my face. Jose had his head looking down, as he leaned on his elbows.

"Mari, it's too fucked up to speak on and I'm going get each person involved." I threw the cell phone and it cracked against the wall. My temper was rising and she knew it.

"Back up Mari." Jose grabbed her away. He didn't know me but I'm glad he had her move. It's no telling if I would've swung off and she caught the wrath of my anger.

"Efrain whatever it is, I'm gonna be there ok?" She leaned in to kiss my cheek.

"If you need me to find whoever, did whatever to you, let me know and its done." I heard Jose saying and nodded. He had Mari gather her things, picked his phone up and sent out a text.

"Dash, is on his way." Mari said and opened the door.

126

"I don't wanna see anyone else today."

"Efrain, we are our brother's keeper and you won't ever be alone again. Remember that." She blew me a kiss and stepped out.

I pulled the covers up and laid there staring at the ceiling. I know killing those motherfuckers won't change what happened to me, but at least it will make me feel better. And hell yea, I'm gonna return the favor. Its only right to give them the same treatment, they gave me.

Dashier

Jose: *You need to get up to the hospital. Your brother is freaking out. His ex showed up and he losing it.*

Me: *On my way.*

I put my phone down and looked over at Genesis and my son asleep on the couch. We were up watching Black Panther for the hundredth time. Evidently, my son is gonna grow up and be the king of Wakanda. He's definitely gonna grow up and be a king in his own right but that Wakanda shit isn't happening.

I lifted him off the couch and took him in his room to lay down. After covering him up, I glanced around the room at all the shit he had already. He had tons of toys, clothes, shoes, the PlayStation and anything else a kid his age would want.

The backyard had a swing set, I had put up before he arrived. There was already a basketball court in the back that he loved to go on. A pool, he had to go in almost every day and he had two power jeeps as well. I wasn't tryna buy him but I missed out on four years so whatever he asked for, I wasted no time purchasing.

Genesis told me I'm spoiling him and its gonna get worse if I don't stop. My mom said the same thing but, in my eyes, all I saw is me tryna make up for time missed. I even made sure to spend every second I wasn't working with him. Gifts are nice but kids need quality time too and I never want him feeling neglected.

"You don't have to leave." I noticed Genesis straightening up when I came down the steps. She's been over here as much as Kingston. I didn't mind because he was attached to her as well.

"He's sleep."

"It's late Genesis and you barely know your way around." She put her hands on her hips.

"I'll have you know, I found McDonalds, and the mall. Thank you very much." I purchased a car for her to get around because I had to work.

"Exactly! A place to eat and shop." She tossed one of the couch pillows at me.

"I'm serious. Don't go."

"Dash, I wanna lay in my own bed. Well, the one I have for a few more days." I heard sadness in her voice as she spoke of returning to Alabama. The month flew by and I knew from the talks we had, she didn't wanna go back. I moved closer and lifted her face.

"You don't have to go back."

"I don't have anything here. I tried to get a job and it's hard to work and live in Jersey. Do you know, I looked online and this state is the most expensive one in the country?" I laughed at how nervous she became. We were close and there was no space in between.

Genesis was beautiful and her heart was pure. She cared for my son without asking for money or even to be compensated. I set her up an account through the bank and transferred funds into it. She cursed me out for doing it but the fact remains, it's in there. She transferred her little 10 k she had saved into the account and so far, she only used a thousand dollars since she's been here.

Now here she is breathing fast as I stared down on her petite body. She had on a pair of leggings with a t-shirt and I noticed her nipples becoming hard. I'm not gonna lie and say she doesn't turn me on because it would be a lie, however; neither of us were looking to be in any relationship.

"I'll get you a job at the bank and you can keep the condo."

"Dashier."

"Don't question it. You deserve to be happy and if staying here with my son is going to do it, then its whatever you want."

"Only if you let me pay rent."

"You don't have to pay anything. Four years of caring for Kingston is your payment." She blew her breath and let her head fall back. She was tryna think of something to say.

"Fine but…" She attempted to speak but my attraction to her overtook the words, when my lips crashed on hers. The two of us let our tongues dance together for a few minutes.

"Shittttt. I can't want you Dash. Fuck!" She backed up with a sad face.

"It's ok Genesis. I get it." She was struggling with Nika being her cousin where I didn't give a fuck. I moved closer again and her back was against the wall.

"You can use Nika being your cousin all you want, but we both want the same thing. When you're ready, you know where to find me." I planted another kiss on her lips and slid my hand in her leggings. Her clit was rock hard, which proved I turned her on.

"Oh God, it feels good." Her knees were becoming weak and she continued kissing me. I removed my hand and stuck my finger, in my mouth to taste her.

"I can't give you that nut until you're ok with us, being us." Her chest was rapidly going up and down.

"I'll do it then." She wrapped her arms around my neck to kiss me and flickered her own clit. I could feel her squeezing me tighter, which meant she's about to let go.

"Ohhhh fuckkkkkk!" She moved her hand and slid to the ground. I picked her up and carried her in the extra room.

"Next time, just wait. I guarantee the feeling from me will be much better." I pecked her lips and walked out. My dick was hard as hell and as much as I needed a release, my brother came first. I locked the doors, hopped in my truck and sped to the hospital. Genesis and I have all the time in the world to explore one another and its exactly what we're gonna do.

****

The hospital tried to give me a hard time coming in because it was after visiting hours. However; I made the lady call upstairs and the nurse gave them permission to let me up. We've been here non-stop and they knew someone had to be there with him overnight. It didn't matter because if they didn't allow me up, he was coming home. Why the fuck do they have visiting hours for grown-ups? This ain't jail.

I stepped in his room and he had the television on but you could tell something heavy was on his mind. I closed the door, drug the chair next to him and sat. I waited for him to speak but after twenty minutes went by I knew he wasn't. Instead of badgering him about it, I took my sneakers off, sat back in the chair and put my feet on the bed.

133

"Nicole came here and brought up me not telling anyone what happened. Mari beat her ass, she apologized and I kicked her dumb ass out. That's after, I hit her in the head with my crutch." I stared at him and let me feet touch the floor.

"Man, I don't wanna think about the shit but it's like I can't get the shit out my head." I know my brother went through some shit in high school but he refused to discuss it. I can think all the things I want, but until he tells it, we'll never know. Whenever he spoke on it, I would listen in hopes he'd tell, but nope.

"When I get this cast off my leg, I'm gonna kill each one; including Nicole." My fists were under my chin and I had my elbows touching my knees. I hated to see him in pain and couldn't do anything about it.

"I may need your help."

"Whatever you need Efrain." He may be the loser of the family but ever since my mom disclosed he's been going through something, my outlook is different. Whatever he went through traumatized the fuck outta him and most likely the reason he's been acting out.

"I want some pain medicine." I stood.

"Efrain, I may not know what happened but taking all these pain pills, drinking and shutting everyone out ain't gonna make shit better." My mom told us the doctor mentioned all the drugs he had in his system and it was a lot. He had some for depression, anxiety, and OxyContin, just to name a few.

"Dash, it's the only way to make the nightmares go away." I sat on the bed.

"No one can help you until you say what went down." He turned his head.

"You don't have to say it now but one day, you'll have to. And I know getting rid of the people is one way to move on, but you'll need someone to speak to."

"Therapy ain't for me." He always says, telling your business doesn't do anything but have people look at you differently.

"Ok then, how about you get a journal and write in it. They say people feel better when they write it down and since you don't wanna discuss it, it's probably a good thing."

"Maybe. You think, I'm damaged? Like, will I ever get a woman to love me for me?"

"Are you seriously asking me this question?" I chuckled and so did he.

"Ma, said yes but pops said, not until I deal with the demons."

"I agree with both of them but pops is right. Efrain you can't be with someone and have mood swings, drink the way you do and take pills. How are you gonna love her, when you're tryna find ways to love yourself?"

"That's deep bro. You should put that in a Hallmark card."

"Fuck you punk. I'm tryna help you and you being funny."

"I'm just playing and I get it. It's hard to move past this shit but I promise to try when I get rid of them."

"Getting better is the only thing you should be focused on. When you breaking free?"

"The doctor said I can go home tomorrow. Mari, wants me to stay with her but I ain't tryna hear her and that nigga fucking." I fell out the chair laughing.

"He crazy about her."

"You don't have to tell me. I saw it with my own eyes earlier."

"I'm glad she found him though." Efrain gave me a look.

"We don't have to worry as much about her because he's there. And don't mention her being with anyone else. That nigga loses it."

"You had to see him when I asked how she could compare if his sex is the best, if she doesn't try anyone else. His face was tight."

The two of us sat up to about three in the morning cracking jokes and discussing any and everything. It didn't dawn on me how much I missed being around my siblings until now. Our absence amongst each other had to be fixed if we planned on staying the tight knit family we used to be. Especially; with my son here and now Mari possibly being

137

pregnant, per Jose. I thought I'd be upset hearing it but like I said before, I'm happy for her and I know Jose is gonna keep her safe.

The doctor came in bright and early the next day, and Efrain asked him for his discharge papers. Once he got dressed, I took the elevator down to get my truck and the nurse would bring him down in a few minutes.

Unfortunately, I ran into Missy, who came straight to me. Aggravation had to be written on my face, and yet; here she is begging for me to fuck her. Crazy as it sounds, I denied her advances and told her in so many words, if she didn't get the hell away from me, I'm gonna throw her ass over the balcony for real. She bounced quick as hell.

I pulled the truck in front of the hospital, helped the nurse put him inside and drove off. I thought about dropping him off at home but in his frame of mind, he needs to be around family. I took him to my parents and shockingly my son, opened the door. Genesis must've dropped him off this morning, but why? Its early and usually he's lounging around watching cartoons at this time of day.

I gave him a hug, introduced him to Efrain, who's been in the hospital since he arrived and told them I'd be back after changing. I sped home to make sure last night didn't force Genesis to leave. Shock was written all over my face when the door opened.

Genesis

"What you think?" I said to Dash when he opened the door. He licked his lips, shut the door with his foot and reached back to lock it. The sound of his key fob hitting the table and him kicking off his shoes made me think he wasn't interested in the way I changed the living room.

"I'll be right back." He ran up the steps and slammed the bedroom door.

After making myself cum in front of him last night, I went straight to sleep. Not only did it feel good but knowing we were attracted to one another is a problem. One... Nika is my cousin and I'm not the type of woman to sleep behind my family. And two... I didn't wanna confuse Kingston either. His little mind is very fragile at his age and the last thing he needs to see, is us kissing or touching on one another.

Kingston woke me up bright and early, begging me to take him over his grandparents' house. He loved his pop pop, but his grandmother had his full attention. I thought about waiting and went to ask Dash if it were ok. I went to his opened bedroom door and noticed the bed was untouched. A ping of jealousy swept through me because of how he left. We were almost about to have sex and he left me to be with another woman. I had no right to be upset but I was, which is why I dropped Kingston off, came back to shower, and started to straighten up.

Of course, I grew some sort of feelings towards Dash and I assumed he felt the same but maybe not. Being around someone day and night, talking and learning about the other can make you feel things you don't want to. Shit, my plan was to stay in the condo and look elsewhere for a new place. However; Kingston wanted me here everyday, so I stayed and became attached to a man, who should be off limits.

I plopped down on the couch tryna decipher if I should move the living room furniture back the way it was. The previous set up was nice but you couldn't really see the television if you sat on the loveseat. The end glass tables were in the middle of the floor and the coffee table was off to the side. It was weird and I assumed making a change is good but I'm thinking, I should have asked first. Changing rooms around relaxes me and it did at the time.

"Why did you change it?" He stood there with water dripping down his body. His basketball shorts clung to his body, showcasing the print, as he used the towel to dry his wet hair.

"Ummm… it relaxes me." My ass was stuck staring.

"You look nice." The devious grin creeping on his face had me nervous.

"It's only shorts and a tank top." I pushed hair behind my ear and went in the kitchen. His presence was felt the second he stepped in.

"I'm not oblivious to the way you stared at my dick." He was blunt and my face had to be red. I kept my back to him, yet; felt the goosebumps covering my body as he placed a warm kiss on my neck.

"Dash." He swung my body around and our lips found their way to play again. This kiss was deeper and more intense than last night. Our bodies were pressed against the other and one of his hands fell to the small of my back. I can't even describe how hot he had me at the moment

"Stop fighting the inevitable Genesis." He lifted my body, placed my legs around his waist and carried me upstairs to his bedroom. I've never been in here because the door stayed closed most of the time and I didn't wanna invade his space. He laid me on the bed and I fell in love with the softness of the mattress.

"Let's pick up where we left off." He used his soft hands to remove my clothes and stared at me in awe. I became shy under his eyes.

"You like what you see?" He asked after taking those shorts off.

"Definitely." I sat up and slid to the edge of the bed to give him head.

His dick lengthened in size as I stroked him with a firm grip. His thigh muscles began to tighten up and I could tell he had his eyes on me. I moved him back gently, dropped to my knees and waited for the sound of approval most men made when you had their dick hitting the back of your throat.

"Oh shit." And there it is. My lips kissed the tip and his hand wrapped around my hair for him to get a better look. I

143

winked and wrapped my warm mouth around, pulling him deeper to succumb and release. I started to hum and his head fell back, at the same time the grip he had on my hair, tightened. My desire to have him increased and I wanted him inside me now but I had to give him a release.

"Got damn Genesis." He came down my throat and I suctioned out every baby he had, until he pushed me off and fell against the dresser.

"I want you." He had me get up, tossed me on the bed, spread my legs and ate my pussy like I've never had it done. Manny did a good job but this man was a pro with the tongue. I screamed out when the first orgasm burst right out my body. He sucked all my juices and continued until I couldn't take anymore.

I gasped loudly when he entered me. His girth, and length were serious and I had to get used to it. He thrusted harder into me, making every pump pleasurable. I let out a deep cry as he hit a spot that brought me to ecstasy. My body became sensitive from the pleasure but he didn't stop and I don't want him too.

He moved my legs to the top of my head and gave me the same amount of satisfaction. The deeper he pushed, the more I came. I tried to have some control but he took over, flipped my body and ate my ass. I ain't never had that done and its sad to say, I'm gonna want it all the time because the feeling is beyond explainable. He tried to enter me but I stopped him and had him lie down.

"Shit Dash. Every position with you is good. Got damn." I moaned sliding up and down his shaft. I enjoyed watching his dick bury itself in me.

"You feel good too Genesis. Fuckkkk!" He tried to grab my waist.

"Let me have a little control baby." I moved his hands and leaned in to kiss him.

"Do your thing ma. Make this dick cum for you." He smacked my ass, sat on his elbows and watched me do my thing.

"Yea, like that. Pop that pussy ma. Shit, it looks good swallowing my dick." He bit down on his lip and I lost it.

"Fuck, fuck, fuck." I shouted and leaned back to play with my clit as I went up and down.

"That's sexy as fuck. I'm about to cum." I went faster and he moved my hands to circle my clit.

"Yes, yes, yesssssss." I could feel my juices shooting out.

"Got damn Genesis. Mmmmmm, fuck." He lifted me up fast and not even five seconds later, his cum was covering my stomach. I reached down, let some of his nut get on my fingers and stuck them in my mouth.

"You should've let me swallow." He had his arm over his face.

"They'll never be a time when you have to ask for it. Take what you want." I climbed on top of him, kissed him aggressively and grinded my soaking wet pussy on his dick. He began to harden under me and I smiled.

"You're about to get yourself in trouble." His hands squeezed my ass.

"It's trouble I wanna be in, if you're the one putting me in it." He flipped me over and entered me fast.

"As long as you stay here, I'm gonna always have this good ass pussy in trouble. It's the punishment, you won't be able to handle." I wrapped my arms around his neck, as he went in and out slowly.

"I'll make sure you put me on punishment next time." He smiled and the two of us gave each other pleasure all day, afternoon, fell asleep and went back at it at night. Thankfully, his mom kept Kingston, otherwise; we would've had to stop and I needed this pleasure.

****

"Wake up Genny." I heard in my ear. I took my time opening my eyes because I'm sure the sunlight is busting through the windows.

"What you need Kingston?" I sat up and scooped him in the bed.

"Why are you in my daddy's bed?" I totally forgot to get up and go in the other room.

Ever since Dash and I took it there sexually a week ago, we've been under each other at home. At night, whenever Kingston went to sleep, either he'd come in the room I stayed

147

in or vice versa. Twice he came to my place because I refused to go over his house. It was no particular reason, I just wanted some space from his. I loved the condo he got for me. We tried to keep his son in the dark but today I fucked up. Shit, he had me cumming so much last night, I fell asleep before washing up.

"Ummm, daddy made me watch a scary movie and I didn't want the monster to get me."

"Did my dad save you from it?" I saw Dash cracking up.

"No, the monster definitely got her, but your dad saved her. I made sure she slept good too." I covered my mouth to keep from laughing.

"Good because monsters are scary."

"They are."

"She's definitely scared of this monster."

"DASHIER DAVIS!" I couldn't hold it in any longer.

"Why are you yelling Genny?" I stood him up and almost removed the covers.

"I don't think you should take those covers off."

148

"Why not daddy? She has clothes on." I did have a tank top on and that's only because I hated to sleep without a bra. I glanced under the covers when he picked Kingston up and I was naked. Dash turned to look at me and laughed.

"Let's go downstairs with grandma."

"Grandma! Dash, your mother is here?" He winked and told me to hurry up and get dressed because she wanted to speak to me.

"Kingston, tell grandma I'll be right there." He put him down and I heard his feet running down the hall.

"That pussy is gonna be next to me every night from now on." I reached over to turn the shower on.

"Dash, why didn't you tell me she was here and wait! What did you say?" I stepped in and had him join me.

"You heard me." His shorts hit the floor.

"You've been here a over a month now. We know so much about one another, you love my son, we crossed the line and have sex all the time. The only thing left to do is make shit official."

"But you used to be with my cousin and…"

149

"And she used me and kept my son away. Genesis, I understand the code women have because men have one but she and I were years ago. You can't tell me there's not some sort of feelings in there for me." He pointed to where my heart is.

"It is but…"

"No buts. You're my girl now and if you sleep with any of my siblings, I'm gonna kill you." I smacked him on his arm.

He explained how his brother slept with Nika and he recently found out when she blasted, he could be the father. I did say he should've let his brother tell him what really happened. If they're as tight as he says, I don't think it's the way Nika made it seem either.

"I'd never risk losing this good ass dick. Matter of fact, let me relax you." I got on my knees and pleased him. His moans were low due to his mom and son being here, but I could still hear him. After he came, I stood up and stared in his eyes.

"Don't cheat on me Dash."

150

"Never. As long as you ride for me, I'm gonna ride for you." He pecked my lips and bent me over. I tried not to yell but it was no use. He covered my mouth the best he could and I prayed his mom didn't hear me.

"I don't know if I can have kids Dash." He stopped putting on his sneakers.

"I have a son Genesis and miscarriages don't mean you won't ever have kids. Like your mom said, he wasn't the right nigga to give kids to."

"But…"

"Kids are in the future anyway. We're having fun right now but if we get to a place where we wanna have some, we'll discuss it then. Just enjoy this ride baby." He kissed my lips.

"You know I do." He smirked and told me to get dressed before his mom came up and got us. Yea, he's definitely a good man. How Nika fucked up, is beyond me. Oh well, her fuck up is my gain and cousin or not, it's been years.

Dashier

I understood wholeheartedly why Genesis was reluctant to be my girl. I've been with her cousin and even made plans to marry her but just like her nigga wasn't any good for her, Nika definitely wasn't good for me. It's unfortunate they shared the same blood, and had our breakup been on some not working type shit, I probably wouldn't even be thinking about Genesis in that way.

I say that because Nika is the one who pushed us together. She never allowed me to meet her family, had my son and kept him away. I hated her with every ounce of my body. By no means, am I with Genesis for revenge.

This woman is very smart, she had a good head on her shoulders and our connection was strong from the minute we met. Neither of us expected to get this far but everything happens for a reason. Say what you want but the two of us were supposed to meet.

She had a lotta doubt about being with me because of her cousin and the fact she believed her insides were messed up. Men don't realize when a woman is carrying, every bit of stress, depression and other mood swings can take a toll on their body. From what she told me, Manny had a lot going on and is the reason she couldn't carry long. It pissed me off to hear he accused her of being with me and saying she'd never have my kids. Only weak niggas do shit like that.

"What if she doesn't like me?" Genesis grabbed my hand going out the room.

"She'll love you, the way I do." She stopped.

"You love me?"

"Not yet but I see us getting there." He turned my face to kiss him.

"I know you love me though." We walked down the steps.

"I never said that."

"You don't have to. It shows in your actions, facial expressions and the way you gave your body to me. It's hard to believe you'd make love to a nigga you don't love." She rolled her eyes.

"You make love to me but you don't love me." We got to the bottom of the steps.

153

"Let me be clear on what goes on in the bedroom." I had her against the banister.

"I fuck and have sex with you."

"The difference?" She folded her arms.

"The difference is, when I make love to you, you'll know."

"And how is that?"

"Because I'm gonna tell you."

"Dash."

"Yes, I go slow with you and you cum a lot but wait until your body succumbs to an orgasm that makes a tear leave your eye, or when your body can't stop shaking. I may even have you come to my office and make love to you, with the city lights beaming down on your body. And last but not least." I ran my index finger over her lips.

"When I put my daughter or son in you, you'll know for sure." She had a satisfied but unclear look on her face.

"In due time, you'll figure out the difference without me telling you."

"WOW!" Is all she could say.

"Fucking and having slow sex is good too but when both of you are in love, nothing is off limits, and the experience is ten times better. You'll see." She leaned in to kiss me.

"You still wanna ride this out?"

"After hearing you speak like that, I'm more than ready." I smiled and took her to meet my mom. If she could get through this interview, she passed the test. My mom has a way to break women down. I hope Genesis isn't one of those weak bitches.

****

"Kingston Davis, what are you doing?" My mother yelled from the kitchen. Hell yea, I had his last name changed to mine. We stepped in and she looked Genesis up and down.

"So this is the woman who took care of Kingston and is now sleeping with his father?" Genesis mouth dropped.

"Don't be silent now. Honey, I heard you from upstairs. Do you know my grandson tried to run and save you from the monster?" I busted out laughing.

155

"Anyway, what are your intentions with my son? Are you trying to sleep with all my sons? You plan on robbing banks?" My mother hit her with various questions.

"Ummm. Where do I start?" She sat on the stool in front of the island and clasped her hands together.

"I am the woman who cared for Kingston all this time and yes, I am currently with your son in a relationship and not someone he's sleeping with. I haven't met any of your other sons and if I did, trust me, I don't wanna sleep with them because I wouldn't risk the bond Dashier and I already have." I liked the answers thus far.

"As far as robbing banks, absolutely not. I don't do guns, and I may not have a lotta money but I have my own. Plus, why would I wanna spend my life in jail over money, I can't even take or spend?" I smiled as she stood her ground with my mom.

"Also, I'm not sure how long Dash and I will be together but I do ask for you and your family to respect our relationship."

"What you mean?" My mother asked and I was curious to hear.

"I'm sure everyone knows Nika is my cousin and Dashier is her ex. However, I don't need anyone judging me on a choice he made. My loyalty doesn't have to be questioned due to me sleeping with her ex because truth be told, we have never been tight and she's done this to me on more than one occasion."

"So, is it revenge for you?"

"If I didn't already fall for him, maybe; but Dash and I spent a lotta time getting to know one another. In some people eyes it may not be enough to learn everything but trust me, it can be done when you're in each other's presence every day."

"Hmph."

"Hmph, what?" I asked my mom and she smirked.

"I like her for you Dashier."

"Excuse me." Genesis asked my mother why she said that.

"You put me through a test with your mother Dash? Are you serious? I thought she asked because she was concerned. You know what?"

"Honey, no man wants a woman his family can't get along with. It causes problems within and my kids are tight, regardless; of this little mishap with Nika. No one is going to come in and disrupt their bond. So yes, he had his mom come in and make sure you were worthy. When you have a child of your own, you'll do the same."

"I understand and I also want you to know that I didn't come to be with him. I…"

"You don't have to explain yourself to me. Just don't hurt my son the way the other bitch did and we'll never have a problem" Genesis nodded and ran outside with Kingston who came in to get her.

"She's a good one son."

"I think she is too but the nigga she left behind is gonna be a problem." I told her about the Manny character.

"Then get rid of the problem and let her live free. Otherwise; he's gonna come for her and when he finds out she's with another man, he may do more harm to her."

We watched Genesis and Kingston on the swings outside. You could see the love each of them had for the other. My mom asked if she wanted to adopt him and even if I wanted her to, ain't no way Nika is gonna allow it. Once she finds out about us being a couple, all hell is gonna break loose as is.

Genesis went down the slide with Kingston on her lap and when they fell off, I laughed my ass off. My mother told me to go check on them. By the time, I made it out there, they were getting off the ground and she was chasing him. I grabbed her waist and kissed the back of her neck. Kingston came running over and stopped in front of us.

"Is Genny gonna be my mommy now?" I let her go and Genesis kneeled in front of him.

"You have a mommy Kingston, but I'll always be the cousin who will love you and let you sleep over whenever you want."

"Yea, but daddy kissed your neck. When grown-ups kiss it's because they're gonna be a mommy and daddy." I sat down next to him and pulled him on my lap.

"Kingston, Genesis and I like one another and she'll be around all the time but I don't want you thinking she'll replace your mother."

"I don't have a mother." We both looked at him.

"Why do you say that?"

"Because I have never met her and grandma says she's a whore and loser. I don't want her as my mother. Genny can be my mommy." Genesis was hysterical laughing, while I glanced at the house wondering if my mother knew he told me. Not that she'd care but why in the hell is she telling a four-year-old that?

"I have to talk to grandma about that."

"Ok. Daddy, are you and Genny gonna have a baby and get married?"

"Kingston, you're asking too many questions. Go in the house with grandma." I let him up and leaned over to kiss Genesis.

160

"We gotta watch what we say around him."

"We?" She pointed to herself.

"Your mother is the one who has to be watched." She got up laughing and reached out to help me. I pulled her on top of me and placed my hands behind my head, staring at her. She let her head rest on my chest, like she was listening to my heartbeat.

"I am in love with you Dash but I'm scared."

"I know and I'm gonna do everything I can, to make you live as free as I do." She turned to look at me.

"We have all the time in the world ma. I ain't going nowhere."

"You better not." I felt her hands sliding in my sweats.

"My mom can see you."

"I just wanna touch. I'm so addicted to this dick already." I smiled and moved her hand.

"He's addicted to you too. Come on." She stood and waited for me to go inside. Kingston came to the door and said, he wanted her to help him and his grandmother make cookies.

161

I'm glad she made a good impression on my mother. Good as her sex is, I would've hated to let her go.

Jocelyn

"What up chica?" I turned around in Starbucks and saw Dutchess. She used to be cool as hell but the bitch became a cop and obsessed over my brother.

"Hey." I grabbed the latte from the girl and stepped to the side. I was on my way to the doctors and didn't wanna be late.

"Where's your brother?"

"Home with his girl." I gave her a fake smile and walked out the door. She tried to speak on it but I hopped in my car and peeled out. What she thought he didn't tell me what went on the night she tried to come for Mari. I had no idea she came to the house because after Jose told Talia to leave my room, and I saw her get her ass beat, I slammed my door and turned the radio up.

The next day, he told me what happened when he returned from the hospital. Evidently, Mari's brother got jumped and almost died or some shit and so did her other, brother's boyfriend. When Jose described what her brother's man, mother and father did, I wish I could've been there to beat the mother's ass.

Regardless; if I knew him or not, I hated when parents judged their child over a choice they made. Shit, if my kid decided he or she wanted to be gay, I'd be all for it. That shit is not a phase and the more people try and hide from it, the more it shows.

I parked at the OB/GYN office, turned my car off and went inside. I signed in, sat down and picked up one of the magazines. This is a moment, I would've loved my mom to encounter with me. However; she loved alcohol more than anything and I learned addicts have a hard time kicking habits.

I blamed her in the beginning, then I stopped because I was harboring a lotta hate and it consumed me. Jose on the other hand, could care less because he made sure to jump in and take over.

"Yea, the bitch thinks she cute." I didn't wanna lift my head and see who was talking reckless but the nosy me, did anyway. I sucked my teeth and wished, I listened to myself and not gave them the attention.

"I don't know why because Rakim is constantly in my bed. If she was all that, he wouldn't have kept fucking me." I slammed the magazine on my lap, rose to my feet and strolled to the other side of the waiting room. There were only a few other women in here and I gave zero fucks.

"Let me tell you something, you dirty pussy, disease giving out, trifling ass bitch." I felt all eyes on me at the moment. It could be because I wasn't quiet.

"I don't go around fucking with you so I expect the same from you, or I'll be forced to knock your stupid ass out again."

"Bitch, you didn't tell me she hit you." Talia said.

"And I'm sure you didn't tell her Mari beat your ass and my brother threw you out naked."

"What the fuck ever?" Talia waved me off.

"Stop playing with me Ranisha. And what kinda name is that anyway? Ghetto ass bitch." I turned to walk away and made sure, to keep my eye on her. Really, I didn't trust either of them.

"Ms. Alvarado, the doctor is ready to see you now." I dropped the magazine on the chair and stared at those two hating ass bitches.

"Keep your legs closed, dirty ho." Ranisha pretended to come for me. I stood there with my arms crossed.

"Next time bitch." I had to laugh. She ain't want none of this with her scary ass.

The nurse closed the door and led me in a room and had me remove my clothing. This is my second appointment and I couldn't wait to get started. At the initial appointment, I was still devasted over Rakim cheating that I didn't even bother getting an ultrasound, snatched the prescription for prenatal vitamins and left.

I sat on the table thing when I finished and text Mari, to see how her brother was doing. Jose said, she was taking it hard. Evidently, something happened to him prior to the fight and he refused to speak on it, which made her upset. I loved the bond she held with her siblings. I'd say Jose and I are the same in a sense. We are all we have and won't let anyone come for us.

"Excuse me sir, but you can't walk in every room without permission."

Please don't let it be who I think it is. Is what I said to myself as the nurse could be heard yelling outside the door. God didn't answer my prayer and this nigga busted in and closed the door.

I hated how good he looked. His fresh haircut and beard was perfect and his swag stayed on point. He looked me up and down and had a sad, yet; satisfying smug on his face. I guess he would, being this is the first time we've been seen each other since he gave me something. He had no idea I kept the baby and I planned on keeping it that way but too late now.

"Sir, you have to leave before we call the cops." The nurse appeared nervous as shit.

"I'm not going anywhere until I see my child on this damn screen." She glanced over at me and I nodded my head yes. If I made him leave, he'd cause more of a scene and I had enough drama for the day. The nurse closed the door and he moved closer.

"Stay away from me."

167

"Jocelyn, I've been tryna speak to you and apologize." My eyes got big. He never says sorry and his arrogant behavior made him believe he didn't have to.

"I was dead ass wrong for sleeping with you and her. You were in a committed relationship with a nigga who couldn't and refused to commit."

"Rakim, this is not the place." He kept going anyway.

"It's not that I didn't want to, it's that I never had to and the first chance a woman I fell for wanted it, I fucked up." He came closer.

"Baby, I'm so fucking sorry for hurting you and risking both of our health for pussy on the side. If I could take back the hurt and pain I caused, I would." I sat there letting the tears roll down my face. Here is a man who loved being a ho, and ignorant; apologizing for hurting me.

"I don't want you to get rid of the baby and if you don't ever wanna be with me again, I get it but don't abort my kid." He wiped my eyes.

"Did I not satisfy you?" He lifted my head.

168

"You shouldn't even have to ask that question but I understand why you did. To answer it, you did more than satisfy my sexual needs Jocelyn. You made me feel things for a woman, I never felt and that shit is scary. It's not an excuse but I also didn't know how to handle the way I was feeling and instead if discussing it with you, I dipped out tryna hide them."

"How did you know I was here?" He showed me a text message from Ranisha saying she was gonna beat my ass if he didn't hurry up and get here.

"You know damn well she wasn't beating shit."

"I do and its exactly why I came because it meant you were still pregnant. I wasn't about to let her make you lose my first child or any child for that matter." I wiped my nose with the back of my hand. He went over to the sink, wet a few paper towels, put soap on it and washed my hands. He gave me more to clean my face.

"Is everything ok in here?" The doctor poked her head in.

"Yes, I'm ready to see my baby."

"You didn't see the baby yet?" I shook my head no and told him why. You could tell he felt bad.

"So you are four months Ms. Alvarado and the baby is healthy as far as I can see." She showed us different parts of the baby and printed out photos for both of us. He was more excited than I was and couldn't wait to let his family know. The doctor had me get dressed and we walked out at the same time.

"Rakim, how you in there with her and I called?" Ranisha stood outside the clinic with an attitude.

"What I do with her is none of your fucking business. Keep it moving bitch before I beat your ass again."

"Again?" I questioned on the way to my car.

He told me how she admitted to giving him the disease and claimed to get it all the time. He punched her in the face and drug her out his house. I laughed because he always said he'd never lays hands on a woman but then again, she ain't no woman. At least, not a real one. Who the hell goes around giving out diseases and jokes about it? He opened the door when I unlocked it and stood there as I sat down.

"I miss you Jocelyn." I started the car.

"Rakim." He kneeled down next to me and smiled.

"I fucked up and I don't blame you for not wanting to be bothered. Can we start over?"

"Start over?"

"Yea, let me take you out on a date." I smiled because he was trying.

"A date Rakim?"

"Yes, a date. You know where two people go out together and do things."

"I'll think about it." He leaned over and pecked my lips. I wanted him in the worse way but there's no way, I'd go there with him. I'm not saying ever because I still have feelings for him but sex is not an option.

"Don't think too hard. I'm missing you something serious." He closed the door and when I rolled the window down he slid a piece of paper in and walked away. I heard him peel out the parking lot as I opened it. I glanced over it and he had a negative status to all his STD tests, as well as the HIV one. I appreciated him showing it because that bitch was scandalous but he still ain't getting none.

****

"Rakim, I'm gonna cum again." Ok, so I slipped up and went to see him after the doctors.

"Then do it." He stuck two fingers in my pussy and I exploded on his face. He slurped, sucked and cleaned everything I had up. He placed kisses up my body and began kissing me like it would be our last time.

"Umph. Shit Jocelyn." He moaned out after entering me. Hell yea, I made him wear a condom. Until he got checked again, we weren't having unprotected sex. The test he took is relevant but it was a while ago. I don't know who he slept with once he took it and I had to be careful. I doubt he'll be reckless again but you never know. I thought he'd have an issue with it but nope. He complied without any problems and I'm happy, because a bitch was horny.

"I missed you so much Rakim." He smiled and lifted my legs on his shoulders. The force he used to drill in my pussy was strong. I felt everything he wanted me to and ended up shedding tears, that he kissed away. What is it about women crying during make up sex? I guess emotions can't be turned on and off.

"I'm sorry Jocelyn and if you need to hear me say it everyday, I will."

"Oh shit, I'm about to. Oh fuck!" I released on him again and he flipped me over to ride. I guided myself down and sat there staring at him. He was so got damn sexy and the way he rubbed my stomach made me smile.

"Go slow so you don't hurt my baby." He wouldn't let me fuck him hard and it pissed me off. I ended up standing on my feet and doing it anyway. He tried to stop me until that current started ripping through his body. His eyes were rolling as his body tensed up.

"Cum for your baby mama." I flicked my clit and went faster. He squeezed my thighs and set his seeds free in the condom, while all my juices shot out on his stomach. I fell back on the bed and felt him get up.

"You good?" He came in with a warm wash cloth and cleaned me up. When he finished, he laid next to me and scooted closer.

"I know you need time and I'll give it to you but I'm not leaving you alone." My head was on his arm and a few tears fell.

"Stop crying baby. I promise not to hurt you again."

"I need time."

"But how much because it's been two months and..." I laughed.

"What?"

"How do you know how long it's been?"

"When you miss someone as much as I missed you, days go by slow and you have no choice but to count them." I turned to face him.

"When you show me the new tests results, we can talk."

"I'm not worried about that because no other woman can say we slept together. It didn't even feel right speaking to chicks in the bar and taking them home was a no, no."

"If and it's a big if. If I decide to take you back and this happens again, I'm gonna shoot your fucking dick off and move away with our baby."

"DAMN! All that?"

"Yup now cuddle with me so I can go to sleep. I haven't slept well in a long time." I told him and he did it.

"I haven't either ma." He kissed the top of my shoulder and both of us were knocked out.

Talia

"I'm over this bitch." Ranisha said when we left the doctor's office. She was mad as hell because she sent a text to Rakim thinking he'd come and black on Jocelyn and it backfired. He came out the room smiling hard as hell with her by his side. I may not be college educated but that nigga is definitely in love. Ranisha can play like she's blind to the fact but anyone could see it.

"You over what?" I started my car and backed out the parking space.

"Over him treating me like shit. I fucks and sucks him well. How the fuck he tryna play me?" Sometimes I wanted to smack the hell outta her for being dumb.

"Didn't you give him a disease?" I turned the blinker on to make a right and she almost made us crash turning the steering wheel in the other direction.

"What the hell you doing?"

"Follow her. I wanna see where she's going?"

"Ranisha why do you even care?"

"Because the bitch claims I'm dirty and he and I were sleeping together. I wonder if she's still gonna fuck him."

"Ok. Again, why do you care?"

"Just go." I shook my head at how stupid she sounded but I'm no better because I followed her.

Jocelyn stopped at one of the convenience stores, went in and came out. She hopped back in the car and pulled up not too long after, at this huge house. I assumed it was Rakim's because Ranisha was steaming mad. Tears began rolling down her face and she tried multiple times to get him to pick up the phone. When he didn't, she finally told me to pull off.

"It's ok. Well both find new niggas and floss on they ass."

"I don't want a new man. I want him."

"Didn't you just tell me about some new dude you met and he gave you the business?" Ranisha ain't no damn saint and always kept niggas in the side. I don't even know why she's this mad over him choosing Jocelyn.

"Not the point and he ain't dishing out the kind of money Rakim is." I shook my head and we drove the rest of the way to her house in complete silence.

I understood why she felt the way she did because I had the same feeling towards Jose. Granted we were never a couple but he never rejected me if I was naked, until this bitch Mari came around. It's like she cast a voodoo spell or something on him.

He blocked me from calling him, cursed me out when he saw me and when I laid in his bed waiting for him, he threw my ass out. I even tried to be funny and make Mari think we slept together but he shut it down. To make matters worse, some chick came back to reclaim him and he was about to shoot her over Mari. I'm gonna get him back in bed, if it's the last thing I do.

****

"You like getting your ass beat?" I turned and saw Jocelyn coming out the store. I ignored her and continued waiting by Jose's truck.

"Hello." She used her four knuckles and pretended to knock on my head like a door. I smacked her hand away.

"Don't get stupid."

"Me smacking your hand away for touching me isn't stupid. You may be able to beat my ass but I'm not gonna allow you to put your fucking hands on me either." She thought the shit was funny.

"I swear if this child wasn't in my stomach, I'd beat your ass just because."

"And why is that, huh?"

"Because even after you found out about Rakim and I, you started talking shit with her. Then, brought your ass to my fucking house, pretending I let you in and stripped naked in my brother's room."

"Whatever."

"Oh its whatever because his girl whooped your ass and he tossed you out like a bitch off the street. Now you're running around town like a got damn stalker."

"Ain't nobody stalking him."

"Says the chick standing in front of his truck but let me be the first to tell you this." She smirked.

"I have his truck because my stomach is too big to fit in my car."

BEEP! BEEP! She hit the alarm and a bitch was pissed. I been standing out this store for a half hour and the whole time this ho had his truck.

"Well since you know everything and he's not here, then I can go home." I gave her a fake smile.

"Thirsty ass bitch." She opened the door. If I weren't scared she'd beat my ass or that Jose and Rakim would come after me, I'd run her straight off the road. I rolled my eyes as she pulled out the parking space and went to my car.

"Talia." I heard a woman's voice call me and turned around. I had no idea who this woman was but she was beautiful. I definitely felt some sort of way when she stood in front of me. Her body was like a model, face was beat with makeup and she had on expensive clothes. Who the hell is this chick?

"Who are you and how do you know my name?"

180

"Who I am doesn't matter but I do believe we both have something in common." I folded my arms and stared at her.

"And that is?"

"How about I treat you to dinner and we can discuss it?"

"You don't have to ask me twice. Lead the way." I got in my car and followed her to some Italian restaurant.

We both got out and sat until the waitress seated us. Still not saying a word, we finally got to our booth, and ordered. She made me feel a little uncomfortable staring the way she was. I know she wasn't about to ask me for no threesome because I don't get down like that.

"How long have you been fucking Jose?" I almost spit my drink out.

"I asked because its time he pays for his sins." She and I both smiled and all I can say is, this will be fun.

Demaris

"Damn, it's packed in here." George said when we stepped in my brother's club.

Levi, was very hesitant on either of us attending this big party Jose planned for Jocelyn. He said it was an early graduation party because once she delivers, she probably won't leave the baby.

I thought she had another year but from what she said, her summer and online classes paid off and allowed her to graduate a year early. I didn't even know you could do all that because I damn sure wouldn't have spent four long years in school, that's for damn sure.

"Hell yea, it is. Let's check out VIP and order." He snapped his neck at me.

"What?"

"Bitch, until your scary ass goes to the doctors, the only drink gracing your cup will be soda and water." I rolled my eyes. Between him and Jose badgering me about checking to see if I'm pregnant, I couldn't tell who was worse.

Security moved out the way and let us in the section.

Jocelyn was already there with two chicks I never seen. She

introduced them as college friends. George and I spoke and sat

on the stools overlooking the club. It wasn't that we were being

anti-social but this is her party and we see her all the time.

They met after he got out the hospital, and we all hang out at

least once a week.

"Let's go dance." Soon as he said it, my man stepped in

the club and the bitches were gawking, as they should.

He had on dark blue Versace jeans with the shirt and

sneakers to match. I only knew because I picked it out for him

and my Versace dress matched his fly. He wore his diamond

watch, necklace and earrings. The shades on top of his head

completed the outfit.

I never understood why men wore glasses in the club

but who cares if they look sexy doing it. The guys he had with

him must be from Newark because he did say, a lotta people

from their hometown would attend.

George and I made it to the dance floor and tore it up.

Song after song, we had everyone watching. The only person

who kept my attention was Jose and that's because he made sure to stay close by. He assumed niggas would want me and whether they did or not, he's the only one, I wanted. It's funny how we met working at the bank and now we're together every day.

"Damn, you are the best-looking woman in here." His arms wrapped around my waist and fell on my stomach.

"And you are the best-looking man in here." I turned and wrapped my arms around his neck.

"Must you two cut up everywhere we go? Ughhhhh." George stormed off. He said we do too much and should never go anywhere at the same time.

"You know how he gets when my brother doesn't give him none." He started laughing and slipped his tongue in my mouth. The two of us were going at it like no one else was around.

I felt someone tapping on my shoulder and turned to see Talia standing there. Jose was pissed and put me behind him.

"What y'all two dressing alike now?" Jealousy dripped from her voice and outta her eyes. I loved it.

"Bitch, get the fuck outta here." I heard Jose yell over the music.

"Oh, I'm leaving. I just brought a surprise for your precious Demaris. Remember him boo?" She tapped a guy on the shoulder and there stood Ethan. My first love, first kiss and first heartbreak.

"Damn Demaris, you look good as fuck." Jose chuckled.

"Oh yea."

"Hell yea. Who are you?" He tried to move past Jose.

"I'm her fucking man and you got five seconds to raise the fuck up outta here or we're gonna have a fucking problem."

"Jose, its ok."

"What the fuck you mean its ok?"

"Babe, he's only saying hi. Ain't that right Ethan?"

"I was but shit, you look good as hell and by the way your body spread, I can tell someone hitting it right." I couldn't stop Jose even if I wanted to. Ethan hit the ground hard as hell.

I noticed Dash coming in with some woman and Levi came in behind him. They both rushed over, picked Ethan up and threw him out. Jose gripped my arm and took me in a corner.

"Mari, don't ever contradict, question or even make a nigga feel like I ain't shit in front of him."

"Huh?"

"I told him to raise the hell up and you standing there talking about its ok. You don't do that shit in front of him. You undermined me as your man."

"Jose, you're bugging. I said, it was ok because I didn't want you fighting."

"Mari, I don't give a fuck about fighting for you. That nigga did you dirty and the bitch brought him here to be smart. Now unless I'm missing something, he came here to start some shit and had I not knocked him out he would've."

"You don't know that."

"Ok, so when I told him, I was your man and he said, someone must be hitting hit right because of the way your body is spreading ain't asking for an ass whooping? I mean, its

186

ok for niggas to come from your past disrespecting you?" I didn't say a word because the way he's saying it does make what Ethan said, sound fucked up.

"You still got feelings for that nigga Mari?" I remained quiet. Not because I had any feelings for him but because this bitch was watching from a distance. I noticed her and tried to go for her but he stopped me. I wished she just stayed away from me but for some reason she continues to pop up everywhere I'm at.

"Your silence gave me my answer. I'm good on you Mari." He went to leave and I grabbed his shirt.

"Jose you didn't give me a chance to answer."

"At this point, I don't even care about what you were about to say." He walked off and I was right behind him and outta the club.

"I thought you said we were never breaking up." He froze. When we made it outside, there were a few people smoking and talking. He came storming towards me and pushed me over behind security to keep people outta our conversation.

"I won't ever leave you alone Mari because I love you and you're having my baby, whether you wanna believe it or not. What I won't do, is be with a woman who can't decipher what she wants and thinks its ok to second guess her man in front of an ex. You know Mari." He fixed the strap on my dress that fell to the side.

"When my ex showed up, I went to bat for you, let you beat her ass and not once did I second guess shit you did. I've done everything to make you feel secure and you did the same up until tonight."

"But you didn't let me."

"Like I said, it doesn't matter what you were gonna say, because you showed that nigga we aren't a union. You let him and that bitch know we ain't on the same page and I can't be with a woman like that."

"What are you saying?"

"I'm saying we need a break. Maybe we're around one another too much and…"

"No, no, no. You don't get to fucking break up with me." I started punching him in the chest.

188

"You said, we're never breaking up and now you want to. Hell no! We are stuck together so get used to it." I kept hitting him in the chest and noticed the sadness on his face. He's never seen me this upset over anything pertaining to us.

"Mari, stop it." I was struggling to get away from him. I didn't want him to see me this upset or crying.

"You said, you wouldn't leave me Jose. You're just like him; only he left me for not fucking him." The tears were falling down my face faster than I could stop them.

I broke free, ran off like a kid getting in trouble, hopped in my car and left. He was calling me and tryna catch up but I was out. I know it was very childish of me to leave the way I did, but he didn't deserve to see the hurt he bestowed on me. Why should he? I understand why he felt the way he did and I was wrong but he wanted to leave me over that.

I drove to my house, grabbed a few items and hopped back in my car. I went to the only place I knew he wouldn't be able to get in; my parents. They knew about him but has yet to meet him. With everything going on, I haven't made my way

189

to their house with him. I parked, used my key to get in and went straight to my old room.

After I showered, I threw on a long t-shirt and laid down. My phone was going off non-stop. I picked it up and saw missed calls from George, my brothers, and Jose. Each asking if I were ok and where am I. I sent a message to George and told him I'm fine and to let my brothers know. I went to Jose's name and opened the message.

Jose: *Call me Mari.*

Jose: *Why did you run off like that?*

Jose: *Please tell me you're ok?*

Jose: *I'm at your house. Where are you?*

Jose: *Fuck it. If this is the types of games you play when you're mad, then I made the best decision by leaving you alone. I mean, what type of grown woman runs off and ignores everyone checking on her. Have a good life Mari.* I tossed my phone on the side of the bed and went to sleep. I am being a spoiled brat but so what. He made me this way and now he doesn't wanna be with me. *FUCK HIM!*

Jose

After sending Mari the last text and leaving her house, I made my way back to the club. It was my sister's party and I couldn't leave her alone. Wherever Mari is, I'm sure she's safe, otherwise her brothers would've contacted me; well I hope they would.

It's not that I didn't wanna be with Mari because I meant what I said, about us not breaking up. I felt we needed a break. A break doesn't always consist of wanting to be with anyone else. Sometimes, it's taking time out to realize if the person you're with, is the one you planned on being with forever. In my heart, I feel she's the one but after tonight, maybe she no longer feels the same.

I stepped back in the club and the DJ had it popping with the music and people dancing. Jocelyn was in VIP with her college friends and the dudes I rolled up with, were in another VIP section. Dashier and his people had their own spot as well, so when security came and said he wanted to see me, I already knew it was about Mari.

I stepped in and he introduced me to his new lady, Genesis and I spoke to Levion. George had a snarl on his face and I expected it, being him and Mari are tight now.

"I just wanna know if she's ok?" George pretended not to wanna answer.

"George don't play games. You know we ain't with that shit. Did she text you?" He sucked his teeth and told us she was fine and going to bed. I definitely felt at ease when he said it.

"What happened?" Dashier asked and the three of us stood away from Genesis and George.

"Yup! That sounds like Mari." Levi said and took a sip of his drink.

"What you mean?"

"It means you spoiled the shit outta her and now that you're tryna take a break, she ain't tryna hear it. Now in order for y'all to speak again, she's either gonna find you or make you do something special to get her back and trust me, it has to be real special." Dashier said laughing.

"Don't tell me the other dude had to do the same thing."

"Oh hell no. She could care less about him and he did make attempts to get her back but she wasn't beat. With you it's different because y'all share a lot more than they did. She loves you Jose and I know you feel the same but don't bow down to her." Levi was adamant too.

"Teach her spoiled ass a lesson. Let her know she has to have her man's back in public and anything she needs to talk about, can be discussed when y'all get home." I listened to both of them speak and they were right. As much as I loved Mari, I can't allow her to walk all over me either. She knows I'll jump through fires for her but she has to be willing to do the same at all times.

For the rest of the night, I circulated from their section, to my boys from Newark and back to my sister. One of her friends definitely tried to kick it to me, but Jocelyn shut it down real fast. She told her I'm married and my woman just left but she had no problem calling her back up.

Mari definitely held a special place in my heart that no other woman could; not even Dutchess who just walked in looking fierce. Body tight, hair nice, shoes on point and capturing every man's attention in there. If they only knew how looney she is, they'd run the other way.

"I'm out sis. You ready?" She noticed her too. If anything, my sister was avoiding the drama we both knew Dutchess would bring.

"Yea. Its closing in an hour anyway." We picked her gifts up and the women with her, helped bring the stuff to the truck.

"Thanks for coming ladies." Jocelyn gave them a hug and the one chick who tried to kick it to me, licked her lips.

"If you ever get divorced, call me."

"Bitch bye." Jocelyn rolled her window up and soon as we were about to pull off, this bitch stood directly in front of my ride.

"Whatever you do, don't get out."

"I'm not." She came to the window and knocked on it.

"What Dutchess?"

"Jose, I wanna talk. Can you give us a minute Jocelyn?"

"Ugh no and you know he has a woman, so why you acting thirsty?" She sucked her teeth and leaned on the window. Her tities were spilling out. One fast move and her nipples would show.

"Jose, why are you treating me like this?"

"Let's see. You sent threatening messages to my girl, stopped by my house and pulled a gun on her, made an attempt to arrest her and made it seem like you and I had some special shit going on."

"You don't miss me?"

"Tha fuck is wrong with you Dutchess? You trying too hard and I'm not gonna cheat on her, for you or anyone else."

"From what I hear, she left you tonight, which leaves the door open for a new candidate and why not me?" She turned around and her ass was fat as shit and her pussy print damn sure showed. However; I wouldn't do that to Mari or myself. If I even let the bitch suck my earlobe, she'd probably go crazy again.

195

"Ugh ahh heffa. This is my best friends man. You gots to go." You could hear George talking shit.

"George, where the hell have you been? Bitchhhhhh, I missed you." They embraced each other. I looked at my sister who shrugged her shoulders.

"I been around but back to why you in my best friend's, man's face? Jose, don't make me cut you for Mari." I busted out laughing and so did my sister.

"You know ain't no bitch ever gonna take me from her. This woman here is my ex, who can't seem to take no for an answer."

"If it were any other nigga Dutchess, I wouldn't care but one… she's my best friend and two… she's my best friend."

"Ugh, how do you two know one another?" I wanted to know before I pulled off.

"Unfortunately, my father works at the courthouse and has for years. When she became a cop, we met and used to hang out a lot. She moved away and this is the first time I've seen her since. Now one more time because it seems like you can't hear." He walked closer to her.

"This is my best friends man and she will fuck a bitch up over him, so I suggest you dick ride elsewhere. Thank you and move on."

"She already tagged Dutchess ass in front of my house."

"Oh hell no bitch. You the one she beat up and tried to have her arrested? Say it ain't so." He folded his arms and Dutchess walked away.

"Jose, Mari loves you and I understand why you felt the need to put her in her place but try not to leave her in time out for too long. I do not wanna hear her crying all day."

"I'll try not to but she needs to learn to have her man's back at all times and not only in private."

"Duly noted and I will tell her." He looked further in my truck.

"Jocelyn, you need to go ahead and let me be the baby's God daddy. Shit, you know I ain't having no kids and

Dashier told me I had a limit on having Kingston. Talking about I spoil him too much. Like who says that?"

"Fine George. You can be his God daddy, but I swear if you ever break up with Levi, don't neglect my baby." He started jumping up and down.

"Oh my God, I'm a God daddy. Hurry up and find out what you having so I can go shopping."

"Thanks Jocelyn. There goes my bank account." I didn't even see Levi walk up.

"I'm sorry, he wouldn't let us pull off."

"Yea, yea. Remember what I said Jose. Stay strong when she tries to entice you because she's spoiled so be ready for it."

"I'll try and thanks for showing my sister love."

"Man go head. Y'all will be family soon, so make sure we're invited to everything and trust me, he will make sure we do the same." I pulled off and took us home. Mari is safe and Jocelyn said, she had a good time. Now my ass can sleep.

****

It's been three days since I spoke to Mari and to be honest, I was missing her like crazy. I know she felt the same because she sent *I miss and love you* text messages. One night, she had the nerve to send me a freaky one, which I greatly appreciated. I definitely slept well after watching it. I was gonna call her but like her brothers said, I need to let her feel what it's like not to be with me.

"How you like your new office?" Dashier asked. He promoted me to a different position, making more money. I don't know, nor do I care if he did it because of Mari. All I know is, my sister and I won't ever be homeless and neither will my niece or nephew.

I have to say, I'm happy she decided to keep the baby. Crazy thing is, I still don't know who the daddy is. She says they're working on getting back together and I'll meet him soon. I wasn't fond of the idea with her getting back with a man who gave her a disease and cheated and I made sure she knew it. However, it's her life and choice.

Now all I have to do is make an appointment for Mari and drag her scary ass down there. I know she's scared and hell, so am I. I don't know the first thing about a kid but we can learn together.

"I like it. One day I'm gonna get one like you and your sister." It's no secret she makes a hella lot more money than me and I'm not ashamed. Hell, her pops owns the damn banks. It would be stupid to even assume he wouldn't see his kids well off.

Anyway, this office had a brand-new desk, two chairs, new computer, I had my own copy machine and a television mounted on the wall. I even had my own bathroom, which I definitely appreciated because men are disgusting and I hated to use public bathrooms.

The sight overlooking the city is nice too and the good thing about this is, Mari is on the other side. I don't mean it in a bad way, but more of her not becoming a distraction to me, like she is right now.

"Oh boy. I'm out. Remember what we told you. Be strong." He raised his fist, moved past Mari and closed the door.

"Good morning."

"Hey." I went back to looking at the computer screen to keep my eyes off her. I know damn well she wore this navy-blue pantsuit for me. It's my favorite color on her and the heels went perfect with it. I adjusted my dick when the door locked and tried my hardest to pay attention to my computer but it was no use.

"I miss you and I'm sorry." Her lips touched the side of my neck and my dick began twitching. She turned my chair around and stood there unbuttoning her pants. She slid them down and removed the blazer and camisole. The white panty set she had on was sexy as hell.

"Mari what are you doing?" She reached behind and undid her bra.

"I was dead wrong for correcting you or even undermining you in front of my ex. I don't have any feelings whatsoever for him or any other man besides you." She took her panties off and threw them at me.

"I love you Jose." I smirked and let her undo my jeans because let's be honest. The two of us fucked like rabbits and we both wanted each other. She pulled my dick out, touched

201

the tip of it slightly with her tongue and let it slide in and out the slit.

"Damn baby." My hand moved the hair out her face.

She traced her tongue down my shaft as she applied some sucking each time her lips touched it. She continued playing around the tip and along the outside of it. I had to bite down on my lip to hold in the moan. She managed to get me to let out a silent one though.

"You're driving me insane Mari." I could tell by the way she began sucking that she was attempting to pull all the pleasure out. The more she sucked, the harder I became and when my dick started to pulse and twitch, she swallowed all of me and a nigga lost it. My legs were shaking and eyes rolled. The minute I let go, she kissed up my body and I felt her nectar leaking outta her pussy and onto my soft dick.

"Give me a minute Mari." Her mouth was latched onto my neck as her lower half stayed grinding on my dick, making it lengthen once again.

"Shit, we not supposed to have office sex Mari but got damn." I lifted her up and watched her pussy gobble my man up. Once she hit the bottom and went in circles, that was it.

"Fuck Jose. I love you so much baby." Her breasts were bouncing up and down with her. I popped one in my mouth and let one of my fingers go in hers. She slowed down her movement and seductively sucked on it.

"You're pregnant Mari." She stopped and stared.

"If I am, I'm not keeping it because you don't want me." I rose with us still connected and laid her on the desk.

"I'ma always want you baby and you better not get rid of my kid." I lifted her legs, pulled out and gave her a death stroke. The shit was so powerful, her mouth hung open and no words would come out.

"I love you too Mari. I love you so fucking much." She grabbed my face to hers and kissed me with so much passion, I found myself ready to cum.

"Mmmm, shit." I came inside and laid on her chest. I felt her hand in my hair.

After catching my breath, I kissed her stomach and went in the bathroom to grab something to clean us up with. Once I did, I handed her clothes and shoes to her. I loved watching her get dressed and she know, which is why she put a show on for me. I don't know if it's because I'm the only man whose seen her naked or what but it was a view, I could never get enough of.

"Can I come over for more later?" She kissed me at the door.

"Nope. You're still in time out, but thanks for that banging ass sex." Her mouth dropped.

"Yea, anytime you want it, I better be the only one you contact and I'm not playing." She had an evil look on her face. I opened the door and luckily for us, the corny ass music was playing loud on the intercom. Hopefully, no one heard us but we didn't care if they did.

"Jose."

"I have work to do Mari." She pouted and stormed out. I appreciated the fuck outta her for pleasing me but she still had to learn. Sex is only a temporary fix. She had to be taught a lesson and even though its killing me not to wake up to her every day, I have to show her I mean business. But damn, I want some more pussy. Oh well, I'll take her outta time out soon and get it everyday like before. Right now, I have a ton of work to do anyway.

Genesis

"Ok, you'll be responsible for answering phones, scheduling my appointments and making sure I have car service when attending meetings. I never want to receive a call asking why I didn't respond to an email or phone call. Any and all phone numbers needed are in that rolodex." I looked at her.

"I know its old school but if the computers ever crashed, or the power went out, I still have them." She shrugged and continued speaking.

"I expect you here at 7:30 am. I don't come in until eight, however; it will give you time to prepare for the day. Also, whenever you step into my office, always have a pen and pad to take notes. An iPad is good but people make mistakes on it and I speak fast. Therefore; asking me to repeat myself isn't acceptable. Any questions?" Dashier's sister asked.

"I don't have any at the moment."

"Good. This is your desk, computer and iPad. Someone from tech will be up shortly to walk you through how to use the computer system. Take all the time you need today to ask questions and familiarize yourself with the programs. I have a meeting in at the New York branch, which means I'll be gone for the remainder of the day. If you need me, send a text and if I feel it's important, I'll step out to call. Otherwise; I'll speak to you when I'm finished." I nodded my head to let her know I understood.

"Oh, one other thing." She stopped at the door to her office.

"Yes, Ms. Davis." She gestured for me to come closer and glanced around the office to see if anyone was paying attention.

"No office sex." My mouth hit the floor.

"If I can't do it, then neither can you."

"But didn't you just give my man some in his office?" Dash said quietly. Where did he come from?

"No, I did not and why you watching me?" She gave him the finger and slammed her door. I was cracking up.

"Don't mind her babe. He still has her on time out and she ain't taking it well."

"Umm ok. But how am I supposed to know if you're in love with me, if you can't make love to me in your office, overlooking the city as you put a child in me?" I was definitely in love with him and wanted desperately for him to feel the same. I also didn't wanna rush him to repeat those three words, if it's not how he felt.

"First off, I'm the boss and me telling you I'm in love may happen elsewhere so don't focus much on the office. And its many places I can put a baby in you at." I folded my arms.

"The bathroom, elevator, rooftop and…"

"I can't with you right now."

"Come here." I followed him in his office and closed the door.

"It's gonna be hard keeping my hands off your sexy ass but I do want to lay a few rules down for you." I sat down in the chair across from him. He licked his lips and I became moist just that fast.

"I'm will try and keep my hands off you." I chuckled when he said it again.

"Also, I don't get involved with any issues, that's what personnel is for." I understand.

"Maxine, can you come in here?" He hit the intercom and had his secretary come in. I was definitely in my feelings because she was bad. Her clothes were extremely tight and you could see how attracted she is to Dashier.

"Yes sir."

"I need you to sit in on the conversation with Ms. Rogers."

"Yes sir." She sat in the chair next to me and crossed her legs. I'm sure its innocent in his eyes but a woman knows.

"Are you ok with that Ms. Rogers?"

"Yes."

"Ok. I welcome all my employees no matter what the position and I do have someone sit in with me; mainly my secretary because she's always here. Personnel will do their normal orientation with you as well."

"I understand."

"Ok, First things first. You are to dress appropriately when working here. No low-cut shirts, pants, or outside wear. This is a professional atmosphere and I want to keep it that way." I remained quiet as he spoke. I loved his professionalism.

"Do not entertain or provoke gossip. A lot of women work here and it's easy to get sucked in but if I hear about it, you will be terminated on the spot. Any questions you may have for me, can go through my secretary and any emails are screened before I see them." I nodded. He was silently informing me that if I wanted it send him anything explicit, I couldn't do it through email.

"You will be Ms. Davis, personal secretary/ assistant and if they're any issues with her, human resources should be your first step. The only reason you will be in this office, is if you're about to be terminated. Do you have any questions?" I glanced over at his secretary who seemed to be staring him down. I rolled my eyes and saw the smirk on his face.

"No. If I do, I'll speak with Ms. Davis. Thank you for the job and I hope to exceed my job expectations."

"Have a good day Ms. Rogers. Maxine, get Mr. Waters on the line from the New York office. Demaris and I have a meeting there today and I want to make sure he has everything done before I arrive." She hopped up and switched out the door. I turned to look at him. He had his head in the computer. I closed the door and went straight to my desk to text him.

Me: *Her clothes are too got damn tight and if you fuck her, I'm gonna kick your ass.*

Dash: *LOL! So are yours but I like the way you look way better.*

Me: *Whatever. Keep her ass in check or I'm getting fired for beating her ass.*

Dash: *Have that same feisty energy when I get home tonight. Oh, and you better be in my bed and not the one at the condo. I can't fuck you good in that small ass queen size."*

ME: *BYE! I have work to do.*

Dash: *Now you wanna work. I'll see you later and thanks for the lunch babe. I love the way you cook.* I sent him a smiley face emoji and placed my phone on the desk.

"He doesn't sleep with women at his job." I snapped my neck and saw his sister leaning on her door frame.

"I didn't say anything."

"You don't have to. I saw your face when you came to the desk." She came towards me.

"Three things to know about my brother." She stared down at me.

"One, he's not the cheating type and since you have all his attention, he won't pay mind to any other woman." I smiled.

"Two, he won't ever disrespect you or allow anyone to do it to you. And three, whatever you do, don't cheat on him because that's something he won't recover from, no matter how much you apologize."

"I won't."

"I don't think you will but know if you do, all of us will be after your ass." She gave me a fake smile.

"The only reason I haven't caught up to Nika yet, is because the bitch bounced but I'm waiting to run into her."

"You don't think Dash wants her back?"

"ABSOLUTELY NOT! That bitch could be on her death bed and he won't go see her."

"Do you think I'm wrong for sleeping with him? I mean, it wasn't planned or anything like that."

212

"Genesis what you do with my brother is between y'all and I don't mean it in a bad way." She sat on the edge of my desk.

"I can say you're wrong but then again, I have never been put in that position. Look." She smiled and I turned around to see her man coming in our direction.

"You had my nephew for all those years and my brother is truly grateful for it, actually we all are. Fortunately, the bond you two formed turned into something else and no one can fault you for it. Neither of you expected to end up in bed together but it happened. Genesis don't dwell on the spectators who will judge because most of them have a lot more shit going on in their life than they care to share. If you two are happy, it's the only thing that matters."

"You're right. I love him and…"

"You love him?" She smirked.

"Yea."

"Ms. Davis you left these in my office." He grabbed something white out his pocket and tossed them at her.

"Make sure you get more like them. They have an huge impact on me." He winked and continued walking by. I put my head down as she attempted to hide her panties.

"No sex in the office huh?"

"Whatever." She stormed off and shut the door. I was cracking up when the Maxine chick came over to my desk. She leaned over and I thought her tities would pop out.

"The boss is off limits Ms. Rogers."

"Excuse me." She grinned and shook her head so the nappy ass weave could swing.

"I noticed how you were watching Mr. Davis and now you're tryna get in cool with the sister. Let me be the first to tell you that he doesn't sleep with women at the workplace and even if he did, I'd be the only one." I laughed in her face.

"What's so funny?"

"Look Maxine. I'm new and don't want to have any drama so let me be clear on my position with Mr. Davis." I went to where she stood.

"Mr. Davis is my employer and I am his employee. If there is or was something between him and I, it would be our business." She rolled her eyes.

"I understand you've been here longer and possibly have a crush on him, but I heard his woman is crazy and will cut a bitch so I recommend you stay clear of him or deal with her."

"Bitch, who do you?-"

"Bitch?" I removed my earrings and was about to swing off. I didn't even care it was my first day, this bitch went too far.

"Is everything ok Ms. Rogers?" Demaris came out the office with her arms folded.

"Actually, Maxine here came to welcome and warn me that Mr. Davis is off limits. The only woman he even thinks about sleeping with is her and I need to back off." Maxine didn't know what to say.

"Isn't that right Maxine?" She began to stutter as Demaris gave her an evil glare.

"Maxine, if you approach my new secretary with anymore of this nonsense, I will have you removed and terminated faster than you know. We don't tolerate gossiping, or threats towards staff about sexual favors among employees, especially; the boss, now do we?"

"No ma'am."

"I didn't think so. I'll be speaking to Mr. Davis and inform him of this childish behavior and he'll handle it from there. Ms. Rogers, bring your pad and pen in my office."

"Anything else Maxine?" I asked and gave her a fake smile. She walked off so fast, she almost fell. That's what her stupid ass gets. I put my earrings back on, grabbed the things I needed and went into my new boss's office. It's gonna be a lotta drama working with this Maxine bitch but she got the right one.

****

"Let me find out you were ready to beat a bitch ass over me already." Dash stepped in the shower and pulled me close. I had just got Kingston to bed and wanted to unwind in the shower. I knew he'd be home late due to work and planned on staying up and discuss his fake ass secretary anyway.

"I'm sorry baby but she…" He shushed me with his lips.

"Don't apologize for protecting what's yours."

"Yea, but it was my first day and…"

"It doesn't matter. Maxine had no business approaching you with bullshit and she will be dealt with tomorrow."

"I appreciate the fact you didn't release any information on our relationship because then I'd have to deal with her wondering why I sleep with you and not her. I don't do office romance."

"I beg to differ." He laughed.

"You were mine before the job so it doesn't count."

"I'm yours?"

"Mine and only mine. You have an objection to that?"

"Absolutely not. In fact, I don't know if I showed you how much I really appreciated you."

"I don't recall you showing me either." I let a devious grin grace my face.

"I wanna be real nasty with you tonight."

"No objections here babe."

I can't even describe the nasty things we did to one another. I know my ass was too damn tired to get up for work. He told me I didn't have to go but I don't wanna be the woman sleeping with the boss and not showing up for work. What would it say about me?

I rolled out the bed when the alarm went off and covered him back up. I limped in the bathroom because he did some damage down there and took a long shower. After I finished getting ready, I woke Kingston up for day care and made us breakfast. I placed Dashier's food in the microwave and hopped in the car. I dropped lil man off and drove to work; only to run into this bitch. Lord, don't let me go to jail.

Shanika

I watched this bitch walk out Dashier's house holding my son's hand, like shit is gravy. If you're wondering how I found out where he lived, that's easy. Every knew which banks his family owned, so I sat outside each one until I saw him and followed him from work.

Same thing with finding Rakim. I don't know where he worked but after coming into town a few days before, revealing my exciting news about who the daddy to my son was, I had been riding around town looking for him and when I found him, I followed his ass too. The difference is I can't knock on Dashier's door because he'd probably kill me.

Back to this bitch. Of course, I had an issue with her sleeping with my ex. Duh, she's my cousin and regardless of what we went through, you don't do that. Granted, I slept with quite a few of her little boyfriends in the past. One or two she may have known about and the others not so much. Shit, it wasn't my fault she played the virgin role and they wanted to fuck.

Anyway, I can't say she's actually sleeping with him but I do know, I haven't seen her car parked in the condo he brought for her. Yes, I knew about that too thanks to Manny, who recently got out the hospital and called me looking for her. I can't even tell you how he got my phone number. I actually cursed him out the first day because I didn't know who he was. Once he mentioned him being the one who helped care for Kingston, I had no problem speaking to him.

Come to find out, he loved my son as if he were his own and had been tryna get in touch with Genesis to speak to him. I asked why Dashier beat him up and all he kept saying is there was a misunderstanding and he'll return the favor very soon. So you know what I did? Yup, I hopped a flight to Alabama to meet this man who wanted revenge on my ex. He met me at the airport and I must say he was a handsome guy and appeared to love Genesis. However; the love shit flew out the window, when he took me to their house and fucked me all over the bed and anywhere else we could get it in.

I told you she could never keep a man and after hearing she couldn't give him babies, is the reason he cheated, I knew

220

his ass wasn't no good. A real man ain't gonna leave a woman for something as small as not being able to reproduce. Yes, most men want a woman to carry their legacy but there are other ways. I guess he didn't see it the same and used it against her.

I felt a little bad for Genesis because before she left with her parents, all she ever spoke of was having a family of her own. She loved and adored children. My aunt and uncle couldn't wait to become grandparents either, per my mom. I haven't heard from them since my aunt smacked the taste out my mouth for hitting her precious Genesis. My mom ripped me a new asshole over it too.

Now I'm sitting here in my mother's car waiting for my cousin to come out the child care facility. I wanna know what she does all day because to my knowledge she is returning to Alabama. At least it's what Manny thinks but seeing her pull into the bank Dashier runs, it doesn't appear to be happening. I guarantee he got her a job and the Benz she's driving because that's how generous he is.

She stepped out in a pant suit, with some expensive looking heels, took a laptop bag out the passenger seat, along with her purse and closed the door. I thought about going on with my business but what kind of cousin would I be, if I didn't let her know how I felt?

She seems to be living my old life but like I stated before, I can't be sure because I haven't seen her and Dashier out anywhere. He could be allowing her to stay closer to Kingston because from what I hear, he is very attached to her.

"Good morning, cousin." She turned and sucked her teeth.

"What can I do for you Nika?" I instantly let a frown form on my face as the light hickey became visible on the side of her neck.

"You fucking Dash?" I got straight to the point.

"Nika, I don't have time for this today. Any questions regarding him, should be addressed with him." She moved past and I was on her heels.

"Hold the fuck up." She stopped and I bent down, grabbed her ankle and lifted her foot. This bitch had on some fucking red bottoms.

"What the fuck are you doing?"

"Bitch, you are fucking him."

"Nika, me having on a pair of expensive shoes does not mean he and I are having sex. And if we were, do you think I'd boast about it?"

"What happened to us being cousins and you'd never sleep with your cousin's man?" She closed the space between us.

"First of all, he isn't your man and how many of my boyfriends have you bedded?"

"Oh you focused on the past?"

"Never because I left it all back in Alabama. But let me fill you in on a secret." She smiled, lifted my weave in her hand, snickered and tossed it. My shit may not be expensive but it looked good.

"You have a son who has no idea who you are and asks questions on why you aren't in his life, but all you're seemed to worry about is who's hopping on Dashier's dick. Your top priority should've been making sure your son was ok."

"Bitch, I know he's ok with his father."

"Did you contact him? Have you given him his first hug? He has no idea what the fuck you look like in person."

"That's not fair Genesis. You know Dash won't allow me anywhere around him."

"But I'm your cousin and I could've at least set it up for you to meet."

"Can you do it now?" She laughed in my face.

"Hell to the fucking no. Dash will kill me."

"And why is that?"

"Because he knows just like I do, you'd only wanna see him in hopes of either snatching him away or tryna get back in bed with him." I smiled.

"False but I wouldn't mind rolling around in the sack with him again. I mean his stroke game is serious. Let's not even discuss the things his mouth can do." The way her face turned up only confirmed she indeed is sleeping with him. She wouldn't have made a face if she weren't.

224

"Nika, you and him have years in and I'm sure spent some amazing nights together but I wouldn't get it in my head of you fucking him again."

"And why is that?"

"He doesn't want a woman who kept his child away his whole life for her own selfish reasons. But what do I know?" She shrugged and opened the door.

"Try it and see. You never know. Maybe memories and feelings will surface"

"I'ma gonna do that and any woman he's with will be a distant memory because like you said, we have years in and our sex was always explosive. Thanks for making me remember. I'm going to see him now and remind him just how much we should rekindle our shit." She shook her head and disappeared in the building. If she is fucking him, I can guarantee her feelings are hurt. No woman wants to hear an ex can come and try to retrieve her spot.

"Damn, you sexy as fuck." I said to some tall Spanish dude getting out a Maserati truck.

225

"Bitch, beat it." I heard and turned to see Demaris. She was still beautiful. He shook his head and before I could respond, the two of us were throwing hands. Well, she was because I was caught off guard.

"Let go Mari." He lifted her up and she kicked me straight in the stomach. That shit hurt like hell.

"If you lose my baby, I'm gonna beat your ass." He stood her up and checked over her.

"Somebody got your stuck-up ass pregnant?" I struggled to get off the ground.

"What did you say?" Dude was standing over me, balling up both of his fist.

"Nothing."

"That's what I thought. Get your stupid ass the fuck up outta here." He pushed me and I had to use my hands to catch myself from falling.

"I'ma tag your ass each time I see you for what you did to my brother and nephew." She threw a shoe at me and it hit me on the back of my head.

"What the fuck ever." I talked shit as I ran to my car. That nigga gave me a death stare and it sent chills through my body. Who the hell is he and what type of control did she have on him? I have to remind myself to stay away from her and him but Genesis. I have a trick for her ass. I picked my phone up and dialed Manny.

"What up Nika?"

"How soon can you hop a flight to Jersey?" Oh hell yea, I'm about to fuck all my cousins shit up. Let me get my story ready now.

Rakim

"Rakim, it's time for you to get it over with." Jocelyn said as we laid in the bed watching some flea market flip shit. I swear she watched the weirdest shows.

"He doesn't wanna speak on it and he has someone else now anyway, from what my mother says."

"Fine! I'll go to the bank and tell him myself." She took the covers off her legs and went in the bathroom to get dressed. I hopped off the bed and joined her.

Jocelyn took me up on my offer about going on a date a while ago and even came with me when I went to get the results from my new STD test. They were negative of course, and she finally let me feel that good ass pussy without a condom and a nigga got lost in it as usual. She is definitely going to be my wife one day. The only thing is she's afraid to introduce me to her brother as her man for some reason. Crazy how he does my books and has no idea he's about to be the uncle to my child.

She met my parents the other day when they stopped by and it's when she found out about Dash and I not speaking. My mom was so happy about us expecting, she let it slip that because we weren't talking, I haven't spent any real time with my nephew. I've seen him over there and I wanted to let him come over but no one thought it was a good idea, being my brother couldn't stand me. I don't know why Jocelyn was hell bent on us talking when she never met him. I guess she felt her and her brother were tight and it's how every family should be.

"I hate to tell you this but banks are closed today." I rubbed her belly from behind. She was now six months and big as hell. Like all men, I wanted a son but we decided to wait and be surprised when she delivered.

"Fine! I'll do it when you tell your brother."

"It's not the same Rakim and you know it."

"Maybe not but you want me to speak to my brother and I want you to mention our relationship to yours. The way I see it is, we both have to face the truth." I shrugged and began washing both of us up. She agreed after saying she had to ride with me to my brother's place. It's the only way she knew, I'd do it.

We stepped out, threw some clothes on and drove to Dashier's spot. His truck, two cars and another vehicle were in the driveway. The other one must belong to the chick who took care of my nephew when Nika kept him hidden.

Jocelyn admired his house and even the landscaping. I expected it being she loved planting and shit. I think it's another reason my mom loved her right away. Now she had someone to garden with.

"Here goes nothing." We walked up to the door.

"It's gonna be fine." She pecked me on the lips.

"Control your temper and remember, even though it was an accident, it was your responsibility to tell him first." I sucked my teeth. She was right but I didn't wanna hear it.

Ding Dong! She rang the doorbell twice and we heard the locks click. Some chick opened the door and Kingston ran straight to me. I lifted him up and began tickling him. The woman asked who we were and before I could answer, my brother's voice echoed through the house.

"You better have a good motherfucking reason why you're at my house." Kingston looked at him and then me.

"No cursing daddy." He stepped in front of the woman.

"Hi. I'm Jocelyn and you must be Dashier."

"Hello. I'm not tryna be rude but this nigga ain't welcomed here."

"Why not daddy? He's one of my uncles."

"Ummm, Kingston lets go see if daddy finished making the cookies." The woman reached out for him and had Jocelyn follow them.

"Remember what I said baby." She pecked my lips again and went inside. Dash closed the door but it was still cracked and stood in a stance with his arms folded.

"What the fuck you want?" I didn't blame him for the attitude.

"I came by to explain what really happened."

"Nigga, I don't wanna hear that shit." His face frowned up.

"Nah, it's not what you think."

"Did you fuck her?" I ran my hand down my face.

"Yes and no."

"Why the fuck do I wanna hear about you fucking a woman I planned on marrying at one point in my life?"

"It wasn't the way she made it seem."

"If you stuck your dick in her, it doesn't matter how she made it seem. You fucked her and it's all I see." The door opened and the woman stepped out.

"Dashier."

"Yea."

"Can you excuse us for a minute?" She asked and I stepped away but could still hear her speaking to him.

"Dash we discussed this and I know you may not wanna hear it but you need to in order to move past it."

"I'm fine." I could tell by his tone he was getting angry and I felt bad because she's about to feel the brunt of it.

"You're not fine and it bothers you. Dash, just listen to what he has to say."

"Genesis, this doesn't have anything to do with you."

"It does when I'm the one who's supposed to be the woman in your life. You have or had a tight bond with your siblings. Don't let what she did mess it up."

"I said, I don't wanna hear it Genesis, damn. What part don't you get?" She backed away and I could see the hurt wash over her face.

"I don't get why you're taking it out on me but don't you worry Dash. I'll be outta your house. Give me ten minutes and you don't have to worry about me again."

"What?"

"I understand your issue with hearing your brother and ex shared a bed but what you won't do is talk to me anyway you want, because you're upset."

"If I tell you I don't wanna discuss something then leave it at that."

"And me telling you I'm gone is the same thing. Leave it at that." She slammed the door in his face. He tried to open it and it was locked.

"What? This shit ain't funny." I chuckled at him banging on the door and peeking through the window. Jocelyn sent me a text asking what happened. I told her Dash showed his true colors and the chick is mad.

"Look, it's obvious you have things to deal with so let me get this off my chest."

"Open this door Genesis."

"One night, you were outta town and I was at a party Ced threw with Ranisha. I was tired and half drunk. I went in one of his rooms and passed out."

"I don't wanna hear it." I kept going because honestly it felt good to get it off my chest.

"I woke up to Ranisha giving me head or so I thought."

"What you mean, you thought?"

"It was dark as hell in the room and she's the only one who knew where I was, so I figured it was her. Anyway, she finished and got me hard again and slid down. At first, I thought I was bugging because not only did we always fuck with condoms, her shit was different." He sucked his teeth.

"After maybe a minute or two, I moved the chick off and shut the lights on. I may have slept with a lotta women but I knew Ranisha's pussy like the back of my hand. Imagine my surprise when I realized it was Nika."

234

"So you're telling me she sucked you off outta nowhere and then climbed on your dick?"

"Sad to say but it's exactly what she did. When I flipped on the lights, she was as shocked as I was, to see it was me. I cursed her the fuck out and said I was telling you."

"Why didn't you?"

"Because she was the love of your life and I didn't wanna see you hurt. Dash, I'm your fucking brother and I would never fuck behind you, especially; not the chick I knew you wanted to build a family with. I may be a lotta things but betraying you is not something I'd do with any of my siblings."

"You should've told me."

"You're right and I'm sorry."

"Why did she say you could be the father?"

"Dash, that shit happened a year before. I think she was being spiteful because she knew I hadn't told you."

"Damn, was I that blinded?"

"You were and it happens to all of us. Look at me. I done fucked around and fell for a woman I cheated on, gave her a disease, she left me and now having my child."

"Disease?"

"Ranisha gave me some shit that was easy to get rid of but when Jocelyn found out, she had just learned about the pregnancy. She wouldn't speak to me and changed her phone number. I guess it's my karma for not telling you." Both of us stood there in silence.

"I apologize for not hearing your side but you still should've told me." He and I embraced one another just as the door opened.

"Hi. I'm Genesis and its really good to meet you. Too bad this will be the last time I see you." She had a duffle bag and suitcase behind her.

"Genesis, aren't you overreacting?" Dash took the suitcase out her hand.

"No. Overreacting is me smacking you across the face for talking to me like shit."

"You ain't crazy." I sat on the porch with Jocelyn who stepped out. I hope she ain't because one thing we don't play, is allowing a woman to put her hands on us.

"I wish I was because you deserve it. Get off me." He had her arm in his.

"I'm going to say this once so listen well." He pushed her against the car.

"You're gonna get out your feelings, take all this shit in the house and when Kingston goes to bed, I'm gonna fuck you silly. Then, when you can't take no more, I'm gonna whisper I love you in your ear until you get tired of hearing it. Do I make myself clear?" By the time he finished she had tears coming down her face.

"You love me Dash?" I shook my head. He basically bullied her into going in the house and all she heard is he loved her. Jocelyn had watery eyes.

"You better not cry."

"It's so romantic." I sucked my teeth because he's always been the lover in the family and now she's gonna want me to be the same. *NOT!*

237

"I realized it when you were about to walk out my life. Just that fast, I couldn't fathom the thought of being without you. Genesis, I apologize for raising my voice and talking to you that way. You've been taking great care of me and my son and I appreciate the hell outta you. Don't leave." She dropped the duffle bag, wrapped her arms around his neck and legs around his waist.

"My anger gets bad sometimes and I don't ever wanna take it out on you again. Next time I ask you to let me deal with something, let me be." She nodded and they started kissing again.

"Uncle Rakim, can we go to your house?"

"I think we should take him. They need a moment."

"Dash, do you mind if Kingston comes with me and Jocelyn?"

"Nah, go ahead. She and I have some unfinished business." He let her down, gave my nephew a hug and so did she. I took the car seat out his truck and put it in my car. They shut the door before we even pulled off.

"What you think they about to do?" Jocelyn asked.

"He's about to do the exact thing we're gonna do later."

"I wanna hear you whisper, *I love you* until I tell you to stop." This is the exact shit I'm talking about.

"I tell you all the time."

"Yea but after hearing him say that to her, I wanna hear it a lot." She busted out laughing as we pulled off. We went to the mall and brought him clothes and pajamas. We both knew he'd be staying the night. I didn't mind because at least I got my brother back.

Demaris

"You got one more time to fight with my baby in your stomach." Jose said in a firm and strict tone. He finally took me outta time out after seducing him in the office. I know he wanted to leave me in it longer but it never works out the way he wants. I did miss him and made sure to show him my appreciation.

"We don't even know if I am."

"Lucky for you, we're about to find out." He gave me a smile. I knew he wanted a baby and I probably am pregnant but I won't tell him because his arrogant ass, got on my nerves.

He parked in front of the doctor's office and we both stepped out. My bladder was about to bust if I didn't hurry up and use the bathroom. He opened the door for me and smiled as I signed in. The two of us found seats and instead of sitting in a chair, he sat me on his lap and kissed me.

I was so in love with this man and I hope he doesn't leave me if I am pregnant. Too many men are happy in the beginning and bounce before or after the baby is born. You know they make the perfect promises and disappear when you least expect it.

"I'm not gonna leave you Mari."

"You better not." He rubbed my belly and kissed it. Some woman sitting across from us smiled and laid her head on the guy's shoulder next to her. It is nice to see people in love, which is why I'm so happy Genesis is in Dash's life. It took him a long time to find love after Nika, but it's been worth the wait let him tell it.

"Ms. Davis." The nurse called me and walked us to the back.

"Hey Jose." I turned to see the thirsty bitch of an ex.

"Don't you move." He pushed me in the room and made me do what the nurse asked. I peed in the cup and got undressed.

"Why is she here?"

"Hell if I know. Open those legs real quick so I can shine the light and see what the doctors see." And like the freak I am for him, I did it.

"It looks fat and juicy Mari." I shook my head laughing.

"If she is, it's because you made her that way." He shut the light off and pressed his lips on mine.

"Damn right I did. You wanna cum for me." He moved the sheet and began circling my clit.

Knock! Knock! He stopped and told me he wanted to see it under the light again before leaving.

"Hello, Ms. Davis." The doctor introduced herself, told me I was expecting and put the gel on and let us see our baby. After asking a ton of questions, she stepped out and this nasty nigga locked the door, pulled a chair up and turned the light back on.

"Now let me see you cum under the light."

"Make me." He placed some kisses on my clit before taking me to ecstasy. When I was about to cum, he replaced his mouth with his fingers and watched my juice's squirt out.

"That shit sexy Mari. I'm gonna put a light on your pussy every time I eat it." He washed my pussy with a warm paper towel and helped me up.

"I wonder how that dick look cumming under the light." He grabbed himself and I unbuckled his jeans.

"Are you ok Ms. Davis?" The nurse knocked on the door.

"I'll be right out."

"I got you at home baby." He opened the door and this bitch was standing there.

"Are congratulations in order again?"

"Again?" I heard Jose suck his teeth.

"Oh Jose didn't tell you how I terminated our baby because he didn't want it." I swung my body around to look at him.

"Go head Dutchess."

"Oh, you didn't tell her. Well it's really a funny story. Demaris, is it?" She followed us out the door and into the parking lot. Jose gave me a look not to touch her.

"You see, he got me pregnant and was ecstatic about having a child and spending the rest of his life with me." I stopped walking, when I should've kept going. I know she was bitter and wanted him back which means she will say anything.

But why did she say inside he made her get rid of it for not wanting a child with her? Now she's saying something

243

else? However, he didn't object to any of the information she spoke of.

"We were gonna get married, raise our family and live happily ever after but guess what Demaris?"

"Get the fuck outta here." Jose was becoming angrier.

"He cheated on me." I gasped and covered my mouth in shock.

"Bye Dutchess." He always told me he wasn't a cheater but she's saying different.

"No, I think her hearing we almost shared a child and you telling her the same things you told me is enough to hurt her, don't you think." I had tears running down my face. Not because of him cheating but because she was right. Everything he told her, he told me.

"Were you tryna replace her by being with me?"

"WHAT? Mari, don't let her get in your head." He hit the alarm on the truck and told me to get in.

"Jose did you say those things to her?"

"Let's go Mari."

"I know you were in love with her at one time and I can expect some of the words to be similar. But it's like you repeated the same thing to me."

"And me." I turned to see Talia standing there with a grin on her face.

"No, no, no. Not again. Jose, please tell me they're lying." I felt my body getting weaker as he stood there tryna find the right words to say.

"Mari, let's talk about this at home."

"One more question Mari. Does he tell you how warm, tight and how you have the best pussy ever? I mean his words can definitely hypnotize a bitch." I saw Jose walking towards Talia and her body hit the ground. He turned to Dutchess and before he could swing off, cops pulled up.

"GET ON THE GROUND." One cop yelled at Jose, hopped out the car and shielded his body with the car door. I instantly became nervous for him.

"Hell no!"

"SIR, I'M GONNA TELL YOU ONE MORE TIME TO GET ON THE GROUND!" The cop looked scared to death, which means this is about to go left.

"Jose, do what he says." He paid me no mind and gave Dutchess a hateful stare. I had no doubt in my mind that he's gonna kill her.

"Stop this Dutchess. You're a cop. Please tell them to leave him alone." She had a smile on her face.

"GET DOWN NOW!" Another officer came up with his gun pointed at him.

"Jose, please get down."

"Mari, I ain't do shit. Talia deserved that punch and if these cops weren't here, I'd knock her the fuck out too."

"I know. Just do what they say." He started to come to me.

"Mari, don't believe shit they say."

"Ok baby, I don't. Please stop and get down." I was hysterical crying and out the corner of my eye, saw Dutchess speaking to an officer. Once he nodded, I knew this would be it.

"He should've gave me another chance." She whispered in my ear. Jose went to grab my hand and shit went terribly wrong.

"HE HAS A GUN!" Dutchess yelled out and it was like my life flashed in front of me. Shots were fired and everything else was a blur.

Jocelyn

Me: *Are you excited?* I hit send to my brother who just found out for sure Mari is pregnant. He kept saying she was and now we found out it's true.

Jose: *Hell yea.*

Me: *Mommy would be happy to have grandkids.*

Jose: *Yea she would. Let me go because the doctor is giving Mari her prescription and directions or some shit.*

Me: *K. I'll see you when I get home.* He sent me back a smiley face emoji.

I put my phone in my purse and stepped out at Rakim's parents' house. Ever since we met, his mom calls me all the time. Either she's telling me more stuff about planting or sending Rakim home with plates of food. Not that I mind because she can cook her ass off but I'm not tryna struggle to get my shape back.

I haven't invited Rakim to my house yet because regardless of me being pregnant, Jose is still upset about my baby daddy cheating and giving me a disease. I'm sure it's gonna be a shouting match because I'd never allow them to fight. It's crazy how my brother does Rakim's books and has no idea.

I knocked on the door and his father answered. Crazy as it sounds, Rakim and Dash favor him a lot. He's handsome, tall and charming. He took my hand and kissed the top like a prince would do his princess. It was cute until I noticed Rakim coming up behind him with a snarl on his face. Who would've thought he'd be jealous of his father flirting?

"Don't pay my husband no mind. He is finally feeling like his old self and thinks he still has an effect on women." His mom gave me a hug and invited me in.

"What you talking about lady? You weren't saying that last night or early this morning." I covered my mouth laughing and she waved him off. I always got a kick out of older couples who still have sex. It goes to show age ain't nothing but a number.

"Did you eat yet?" She asked walking through the living room. There was a photo that caught my eye and stopped me in my tracks. I walked over and took a look.

"*It can't be.*" I whispered to myself; well thought I did.

"What can't be?" I felt a kiss on my neck.

"Is Mari your sister?" I asked pointing to the photo of them as a family. Some relatives take pictures together before people say it's a dumb question.

"Yea and those are my other brothers. That's Efrain, Levion and you met Dashier. He pointed to each one individually, so I knew who, was who." I stood there in shock because all this time we never knew they were siblings. I didn't anyway.

"Do you know her?" I hesitated because I remember Jose mentioning Mari being afraid to tell one of her brothers about their relationship because he didn't want her with a thug. I was about to answer when my phone started ringing in my purse. The number was unfamiliar but I answered anyway.

"Hi, is this Ms. Alvarado? The sister of Jose Alvarado?"

"Yes, this is she?" I walked away from the mantle and stood by a window.

"This is Maria from the Englewood Medical center and I'm calling because your brother has been brought in and…"

250

"WHAT? What happened to him?' I grabbed my things and noticed Rakim and his parents staring at me.

"I'm not at liberty to say over the phone but you should get here as soon as possible."

"Oh my God. Is he ok? What about his girlfriend?" I asked because they were together at the doctor's, and if he's there, so is she. But why didn't she call?

"A woman was brought in with him and we're tryna contact her family as well. Do you know how to get in touch with them?" I looked at their puzzled faces.

"I'm with them now. We'll be there soon." I hung up and Rakim came over to hug me.

"What's the matter Jocelyn? You're shaking."

"Sit her down Rakim. Let me grab her something to drink."

"NO!" I shouted and his mom stopped.

"We don't have time to waste. We all have to get to the hospital."

"We?" His father questioned.

"Yes. Something happened to my brother and his girlfriend was with him. They won't tell me if either of them are ok."

"I'll go with you but why would my parents have to go?" I looked at the innocence in Rakim's face and that's when I knew, he had no idea about Jose and Mari. This is the brother she was hiding her relationship from.

"His girlfriend is Mari." Rakim's face turned from sad to angry as he almost knocked me over leaving the house.

"Ride with us." His mother said and they grabbed their things. I hope they have some cops there because shit is about to hit the fan.

Efrain

"Mr. Davis, I'm not going to force you to do or say anything. If you want to sit here and stare at the things in my office or out the window, be my guest." The woman said.

I decided to see a therapist and deal with my demons. Well actually; my parents made the appointment and Levion dragged me down here. And I mean literally. He barged in the house, waited for me to get dressed and pretended we were picking George up from the doctors. When we walked in, he pushed me in the office and told me, he was standing outside the door until I was done.

The woman wasn't surprised at all, which let me know they had this set up for a while. I don't know why my family insisted on me attending these sessions. Dash told me to write everything in a journal and I have. It feels good to get it off my chest but I hate reliving it.

"Oh you tough nigga?" Some guy yelled out.

"Why y'all fucking with me anyway?" I tried catching my breath. Being drunk and fighting takes a lot outta a person.

"You think talking shit is ok?"

253

"Y'all dragged me up the stairs over a chick I fuck with and then, disrespect her. What you expect me to say?"

"Oh shit. You really like her." I spit blood on the side of the ground.

"Obviously, if I'm with her."

"Beat his ass Bobby." The dude walked over to me.

"I got something better. Lock the door."

"Lock the door for what?"

"We doing him the same as the others?"

"The others?" I questioned. These punks must jump people all the time.

"Yup. And I'm up first. The last one was half dead before I got to him." Now me not having no idea what they spoke of, got in my fighting stance but what happened next traumatized the fuck outta me. I wouldn't wish this shit on no one.

"Mr. Davis. Mr. Davis are you ok. Sir, I need you to come get your brother." I heard but my eyes were struggling to open.

"Efrain! Efrain wake up."

254

WHAP! I think the smack made my eyes open. I felt sweat dropping down my face.

"What? What you hit me for?" Both of them were staring at me with a pitiful look. The doctor walked away and I could hear water running in her private bathroom.

"Here you are." She handed me some wet paper towels and tissue.

"Bro, what type of daydream you having? I mean you were beating yourself up." I looked at the tissue and noticed blood.

"Why am I bleeding?"

"Sir, you were swinging and hit yourself in the face a few times. I know we discussed you just sitting here and not speaking but…" She came closer to me and kneeled. She pulled her skirt to her knees to make sure nothing showed.

"The demons you're fighting are only going to get worse until you speak on it." I tried to talk.

"Writing them down is great too but whatever you're dealing with is much deeper and needs to be discussed."

"I said, I DON'T WANNA TALK ABOUT IT! WHY ISN'T ANYONE HEARING ME?" She stood and backed up.

"Bro, we can't hear you because you're not saying anything."

"I DONT NEED TO SAY IT! FUCKKKKKK!" I shouted and punched out the glass window.

"Oh my God." The doctor covered her mouth and Levi looked at me with sadness on his face.

"You think I wanna deal with this shit bro? Huh?" He just looked at me.

"I'm taking pills just to sleep and ease the pain. I'm a disappointment to my entire family and now those motherfuckers are taunting me. I'm gonna kill each one real slow, right after I return the favor." I limped back and forth in the room. The cast was off but I still had to wear a brace.

"Who Efrain? Tell me who and you know we'll get each one and bring them to you." I could hear the pain in Levi's voice.

"I don't wanna talk about it."

"There you go shutting down again."

"Take me home."

"Efrain."

"TAKE ME THE FUCK HOME NOW!!!!" The doctor jumped.

"Is everything ok in here?" Two officers asked. The secretary must've heard glass breaking and contacted the police.

"Everything's fine." The officers looked at her and then me. I put my hand behind my back because there was a deep cut on it.

"Are you sure?"

"Yes, I'm sure. I was trying a new technique with a ball to relax my client and it accidentally broke the window. I'm good." Me and Levi gave her a look. Why did this woman lie for me? The officers stepped out and she came over to me. She handed me a towel to cover my hand and stop the bleeding.

"Mr. Davis, you're upset, aggravated, angry and most of all frustrated and I understand. You want to express what happened but scared of the reaction your family will give you.

257

Let me be very clear when I say this." She placed my hands in hers.

"I've briefly spoken to each of your family members and all of them want to see you get better. They hate to see you going through something and can't help. I have a solution but we don't have to do it if you don't want to."

"What? If you can tell me how to fix this, be my guest."

"I want to have a sit-down meeting at your parents' house with them and your siblings. I want you to lay it all on the line no matter what it is and we can go from there." I snatched my hands away.

"Hell fucking no. I'm ready to go." I walked to the door.

"I'm going to do it anyway." I ran up on her and she didn't even flinch. How she gonna tell me if I don't wanna do it, we don't have to. Then, say she's doing it anyway.

"I don't care if you're mad and if you're wondering why I'm not scared, it's because if you wanted to hurt me, you would've done it already." I stared in her eyes and felt like shit for even thinking about attacking her. She's only tryna help.

"Stop hiding behind the trauma and let it out. The only people who will know is your family and they're not going to tell anyone. Stop giving those bastards who hurt you power. It's time to get your life back Efrain Davis." I had no response for what she just said.

"I'm going to set the appointment up for one day next week." I stepped out the office and heard Levi speaking with her.

Once we got in the car, Levi's phone rang. He told me it was George and he was worried about me too.

"Calm down George." Why is he telling him to calm down? His parents must've did some bullshit again.

"We'll be right there."

"What happened?" Levi was flying down the street.

"We need to get to the hospital."

"Really Levi." I shouted because my head hit the window when he turned the corner too fast.

"Be quiet."

"Jocelyn said, something happened to Jose and Mari was there."

"Is she ok?" Levi glanced over at me.

"I don't know. He just said we need to get there." I laid my head on the seat and waited for him to pull up at the hospital. *So much for going home to kill myself.*

"Did Mari get in yet?" I asked Genesis the fifth time this morning.

"No, she said her doctor's appointment was today. Did you forget?" She told me in the phone and I relaxed a little.

The two of us spoke last night and Jose told me he made her an appointment because she was taking too long and his kid needed vitamins. Mari refused to entertain the thought of being pregnant but he was adamant she is carrying his child. I agreed with him making her an appointment because she wouldn't have.

"I did forget. Do you know what time it was?" She hung the phone up and knocked on the open door to my office.

"Are you ok? Is there something wrong with Mari?"

"Nah, it's just not like her to go this long without calling."

"Maybe they're celebrating, like we should be." I looked up at her.

"What we celebrating?"

"That you admitted to being in love with me." She straddled my lap and my dick woke right up for her.

"What did I tell you about office sex?"

"You promised to make love to me here under the city lights too. Just because you told me at home doesn't mean I don't still wanna do it."

"Whenever you're ready."

"I'm always ready for this." She undid my pants, pushed my chair back and got on her knees.

"Got damn baby." Her mouth was soaking wet and she was swallowing my dick whole.

"Mr. Davis, there's someone downstairs requesting to see you." Maxine said when she came in. I thought Genesis would stop.

"Ok. Fuck!" Genesis had my balls juggling in her mouth. She knew I loved that shit.

"Is everything ok?"

"Yea, I'm just thinking about something. Got dammit."

"You sure, you're ok?" She asked again.

"I'm fine. Do me a favor and close the door on the way out and whoever is downstairs let them know, I'll be there in a few minutes. Oh shit." Maxine gave me a crazy look. I waved her off and hurried her to close the door. My nut was at the tip and if she didn't leave, I can't say she wouldn't have figured it out.

"Let it go Dash." She whispered and winked.

"Shittttttttttt. Genesis, fuck." I gave her a lot and watched as she suctioned it all out and wiped her mouth with the back of her hand.

"Stay right here." I went over to the door, locked it, took my shirt off and placed her on all fours on my desk.

"You wanna play right? You better not make one fucking sound and I mean it." I spread her ass cheeks and dove right in, taking turns licking and sucking on her pussy and ass.

"Dashhhhh." She whispered silently. I let my pants and boxers fall to my ankles as she succumbed to that orgasm.

"You better not get loud or I'm gonna fuck you real hard." She nodded and bit down on her arm when I sat her on my dick, cowgirl style. Her head was lying on my chest as I fucked her from the bottom.

"Fuck me back Genesis." She placed her hands on my legs and popped her pussy the way I liked it.

"Yea ma. This pussy talking to me." She bent over further and I stood to hit it from the back.

"No noise." She nodded her head and I could tell she was struggling to keep the moans in, the same way I was.

"Oh shit Dash, I'm about to cum again and…"

"And what?" I watched her body shake and juices spit out.

"I love you Genesis." I held her tight and for the first time, released my seeds in a woman since my ex. My siblings are having kids so I may as well join them. I lifted her up and sat her on my lap. She was exhausted and snuggled her face in my neck.

"I love you too baby." She put her legs on my lap.

"Mr. Davis, the person downstairs is being rude and requesting your presence right away." Maxine spoke though the intercom.

"Call my friends at the precinct and have two of them stop by. I'll be right down." I'm no punk but when someone comes into a bank requesting to see the CFO, its usually to rob them or some other shit.

"Everything ok?" I walked in the bathroom with Genesis and we cleaned ourselves up.

"Yea, it should be. When I leave, wait a few minutes and come out. Maxine will be with me but until the elevator arrives, she'll be stalking my office door."

"Stalking is all she better do."

"It is sexy. I'll see you in a few." I kissed her lips and closed the door behind me.

"Let's go Maxine." I checked for my weapon and pressed the elevator button. I noticed my sister door was closed.

"Did my sister walk past you?"

"No, maybe her secretary is in there." I smirked because it meant she had no idea someone was with me.

"Oh ok. I'll check when we're done with whoever this is." We stepped on the elevator and she hit the lobby button.

Once the doors opened, I sucked my teeth. Why is this bitch even here?

"Hello Dashier. This is my lawyer, Mr. Collins and I think you know who this is." The guy turned around and I could've beat that smirk right off his face.

"A lawyer for what Nika?"

"My son. You know the one I can't see because you keep him away?" Before I got to speak, I heard Genesis calling me in a distressed tone. I noticed a phone in her hand and a sad look on her face. Something told me it was about my sister but I had to wait for her to speak.

"What's wrong?" I asked and she froze.

"Hello Genesis."

"What... what are you doing here?" Her body started shaking.

"Oh, I was just about to inform Mr. Davis here, how you are going to be arrested for planning to rob this bank." Two officers came through the door.

"SAY WHAT?" I shouted and turned to look at her.

"Oh, Genesis here is just like her cousin. Ain't that right?" Genesis stood there stuck and my gun went straight to her forehead.

"Tell me right now Genesis if you were using me and planning on robbing my bank." I cocked my gun and waited for her answer. When she remained silent, it was Nika all over again.

"Dash." She had tears running down her face. There's no way this could be happening to me again. Does God really hate me that much?

To Be Continued....

CPSIA information can be obtained
at www.ICGtesting.com
Printed in the USA
LVHW080635281019
635474LV00022B/471/P